ANATOMY OF A BOYFRIEND

ANATOMY OF A BOYFRIEND

A NOVEL BY DARIA SNADOWSKY

DELACORTE PRESS

Published by Delacorte Press
an imprint of Random House Children's Books
a division of Random House, Inc.
New York

www.randomhouse.com/teens

Educators and librarians, for a variety of teaching tools, visit us at
www.randomhouse.com/teachers

Library of Congress Cataloging-in-Publication Data
Snadowsky, Daria.
Anatomy of a boyfriend / Daria Snadowsky.— 1st ed.
p. cm.
Summary: In her last semester at a private school in Fort Myers, Florida, seventeen-year-old Dom finds her life transformed by her first boyfriend, Wes, a track star at the public school her best friend attends.
ISBN: 978-0-385-73320-5 (trade)
ISBN: 978-0-385-90339-4 (glb)
[1. Dating (Social customs)—Fiction.   2. Sex—Fiction.   3. Family life—Florida—Fiction.   4. High schools—Fiction.   5. Schools—Fiction.   6. Florida—Fiction.]   I. Title.
PZ7.S664953Ana 2007
[Fic]—dc22
2006016045

The text of this book is set in 12-point Apollo MT.

Book design by Angela Carlino

Printed in the United States of America

10 9 8 7 6 5 4 3 2 1

First Edition

FOR
JUDY BLUME
AND
DOROTHY TENNOV

ACKNOWLEDGMENTS

Humblest gratitude to my editor, Joe Cooper; to my agent, Scott Miller; and to everyone at Random House and Trident for their tireless perfectionism. Deepest appreciation for my professors Dr. Patrick Allitt, for his guidance, and Dr. David Edwards, whose Psychology of Love course exposed me to the pioneering work of Dr. Dorothy Tennov. Infinite love to my parents, Stanley and Michelle, for their unwavering support, and to my sister, Leslie, for being my best friend and introducing me to the world of Judy Blume. Endless thanks to my friends, teachers, and loved ones for their feedback and encouragement, and especially to Allan Pepper, for always making time for me. Finally, this book is in loving memory of Valerie Kay Hardy, who inspired me to write.

ANATOMY OF A BOYFRIEND

PART I

1

My best friend, Amy, wants to wait until college to "do it," but until then she'll do "everything but" with boys she thinks are cute and have good bodies. She thinks lots of boys are cute and have good bodies. One of Amy's favorite activities is scoping out the jocks at the annual seniors versus teachers football game at East Fort Myers High, which everyone calls EFM. It's the largest local public school, and as lame as it sounds, this game is the hottest ticket in town the day after Christmas.

I couldn't care less about sports, let alone ogling athletes, and a school is the last place I want to be during winter break. But I'm tagging along this year because I've been holed up in my room all week finishing college applications, and I desperately need a change of scenery. Not surprisingly, Amy's boy-crazy jabbering makes it impossible even to pretend to focus on the game.

"See him?" she asks me while pointing to one of the senior team's broad-shouldered linebackers, who's also in her woodworking class. "I had this amazingly intense dream about him last night. We were in this, like, psychedelic art studio, and I was posing nude for him—"

"Amy!" I cut her off. We're sitting on the bleachers one row ahead of a pack of pervy-looking freshmen, and I know they're eavesdropping.

"What?" she looks at me innocently. "It was really hot! Then he knocked over his easel, tore off his overalls, and said, 'My canvas is your body, and my paintbrush is my peni—' "

"Shhh!" I almost choke on my hot dog as I press my hand over Amy's mouth. "First of all, gross! Second of all, the entire population of Florida does *not* need to know this." I motion with my eyes to the cackling pervs behind us. "Can you please tone it down?"

Amy tears my hand away. "Oh, c'mon, Dominique. You sound like a librarian . . . and not the kinky kind." She grins at me mischievously before turning her attention to the buff, freckled junior on her right. I just roll my eyes in resignation.

If we weren't in a public place, I wouldn't mind hearing the steamy details of Amy's dream. That's the key to our friendship—we can be open with each other past the point of too much information. She ends up doing most of the talking, though, since she has a lot more experience to draw from. But the fact that I'm probably the only seventeen-year-old in Fort Myers who hasn't French-kissed a guy yet does not mean I'm a prude. My dreams at night can get just as X-rated as Amy's, and sure, I guess I'd like to have a boyfriend. I just wouldn't want to hook up with a guy unless I really, really like him, and in my experience all boys can be classified as either assholes or bores, unless they're both.

Maybe it's a blessing, because the last thing I need is relationship drama to sidetrack me from my grades. Amy, on the other hand, has never been the studious type but still managed to score an early acceptance to Amherst College. She's a master painter and graphic artist, which makes sense given her expressive, exhibitionistic personality. I'm way more introverted.

My biggie Sprite makes itself known a few minutes into the third quarter. I maneuver my way down the bleachers toward the row of light blue Porta Pottis behind the end zone, but when I get to ground level I see I have competition. A chunky mom type with a bulging fanny pack is waddling in the direction of the only unoccupied stall. Nature is calling loudly, so I start chugging across the green, eyes on the prize. That's when I feel my feet slip out from under me, and the next thing I know I'm sprawled facedown on a patch of newly watered grass.

"Shit!" I shout as I scramble onto all fours. I look down at my sweatshirt and shorts, now coated with wet topsoil. I don't care if you're the most confident person in the world—when something like this happens, all you want is the superpower to become invisible.

5

"Jeez, you okay?" a deep voice asks.

Startled, I gaze up through the strands of my bangs, now shellacked to my forehead with sprinkler water. All I see are blazing blue eyes against a halo of high-noon sunshine.

"Um, yeah, I'm fine," I gasp, half-frightened and half-hypnotized by his proximity.

"You were fast. You should go out for track." He grins.

I force myself to laugh. "Thanks, but I think mud wrestling's more my style."

He grins a little wider in a cute, bashful manner. My stomach suddenly feels uneasy, but not in a bad way. I don't need to pee anymore either.

"Let me help," he says.

Without giving myself time to think about it, I reach for his outstretched hand. He clasps my forearm, since my palms are caked with dirt and grass, and pulls me to my feet.

I'm still squinting from the sun's brightness, but it's clear that this boy with the sparkling blue eyes is around my age. His angular features are balanced by his gentle, soulful stare and the shaggy blond hair falling softly over his ears. He's skinny and tall, around six feet. Amy and I are both five six, except I look shorter because I tend to slouch, which my grandma never fails to give me a hard time about.

"Hmmm." The blue-eyed boy crinkles his brow while staring at my legs. "Your knees—they're pretty scratched up. I have some Band-Aids in my car just over there." He looks at me expectantly.

The part of me that's humiliated to be standing there dripping with mud wants to run away. But this boy's rare

6

combination of niceness, humor, and good looks is drawing me in. I can hear a tiny Amy on my shoulder whispering, *Whatever you do, keep talking to him!*

"Thanks, but I'll be fine. Um, so, do you go to EFM?" I ask, going for the obvious.

"Yep. I'm a senior."

"Oh? So why aren't you out there on the field?"

"I'm not into football, but I know some guys on the team, so I'm here rooting for them."

"Cool. Well, I'm a senior too. Not here, though. I mean, my best friend goes here, but I—"

"Chiiiild, are yeew alriiiight?" I hear in the world's most grating Southern drawl. "Ya fell like a rock in a pond."

Damn! It's that fanny pack lady I was trying to outrun. I instantly hate her for jarring me out of my cute-boy moment.

"Ya pooor li'l thing," she croons as she wraps her fleshy arm around my shoulder. "Ah woulda come to ya right away, but Ah hadda go somethin' awful. Those hot dawgs go through ya like a bag o' prunes."

"Oh. Yeah," I respond, too horrified to come up with something better.

"Now, Ah'm a registered nurse," she continues, "so lemme take a look at those legs."

"Thank you, ma'am, but I'm fine. Really."

Oblivious to my brush-off, she bends down to study my knees and in the process displays some major ass crack. The cute boy is visibly grossed out. I sense blood rushing to my face in helpless embarrassment, and all of a sudden my urge to pee returns with a vengeance. It's like I traveled from heaven to hell in the space of ten seconds.

I'm racking my brain for a polite way to tell the nurse to get lost when a breeze streams by, carrying with it the Porta Pottis' pungent stench of human waste. I can feel the puke rocket up my esophagus.

"You sure you're okay?" the blue-eyed boy asks, looking concerned—or maybe just repulsed.

I avoid making eye contact with him as I keep my mouth clamped shut and nod. Then I shake the lady's pudgy fingers from my knees and scuttle to a newly vacated stall. I hear her tell the boy, "Ah guess she hadda go bad too."

Upon slamming the flimsy plastic door behind me, I barf up my hot dog and ketchup for the next two minutes. When I'm done I peer into my compact mirror and groan as I think about the boy's last image of me: a swamp thing racing for a foul-smelling Porta-Potti. Does *Guinness World Records* have a Worst First Impression category?

After peeing I clean my hands, shins, and face as well as the few remaining sheets of toilet paper allow. Then I take off my mud-spattered sweatshirt, turn it inside out, and wrap it around my waist so it's hanging over the front of my shorts, concealing the mud stains. Finally I undo my pony-tail and let my hair fall over my face. Sufficiently disguised, I slink back up the bleachers and collapse onto my seat. Amy's still flirting with the buff, freckled junior, who's punching his phone number into her cell. When presented with a member of the opposite sex, some of us get numbers and some of us throw up.

"Did you fall in?" Amy asks when I tap her shoulder to get her attention.

"Well . . . I fell."

"What the hell happened?" she shrieks, pointing to the dried blood on my legs. Then she picks a blade of grass out of my hair. "You look like one of my smocks."

"Thanks," I say sarcastically, trying to ignore the pervs cackling at me for the second time today. Then I tell her that I just had the worst twenty minutes of my life and I want to go *now*.

Even though I hope the blue-eyed boy can't see me, I can't stop myself from scanning the bleachers for him as we leave. I don't find him, of course, as most of the thousand-plus spectators are too far away to make out. No matter. Even if I did spot him, I wouldn't approach him. I'd be afraid I'd lose my cool again, especially in my current state of extreme fugliness. Why am I even obsessing about this? I never get worked up over guys. Maybe that's the problem— our interaction wasn't long enough for him to ruin his good first impression with the inevitable stupid comment or dude behavior. A minute longer and he would have belched in my face or tried to touch my butt. Boys are all assholes or bores, anyway.

2

"We'll find him," Amy announces confidently as we drive back to her place. "This is exciting, Dom. You met a guy besides Matt who you actually *want to get with*!"

Matt, Amy's gorgeous stepbrother, is a junior at Cornell. He's also been with the same girl since high school. But in a way, that makes things easier—since I know he's taken I've never had to worry about getting him to like me back. Still, stealing glimpses of him sunbathing in his Speedo whenever he's home on vacation remains one of the perks of being Amy's best friend.

"Want to get with?" I exclaim from the backseat, where I'm changing into Amy's gym uniform, which lucky for me

she keeps in the car. "I just said he was nice. I never said I *want to get with* him."

"Well, you should! You spend hours staring at bodies in textbooks, yet you've never gotten off on one. It's just not healthy."

"Whatever." I crawl into the passenger seat. "I haven't gotten sick yet."

Amy loves making fun of the fact that my favorite book is *Gray's Anatomy* (basically the bible of human biology), which in my opinion is a lot more interesting than the trash romance novels she reads. The truth is, I've wanted to be a doctor ever since I played my first game of Operation when I was six, and I'm constantly amazed at how strong and complex our bodies are, especially considering we all start off as single cells and are composed mostly of water.

Meanwhile, Amy's convinced my fascination with human anatomy is really some kind of Freudian sublimation of my nonexistent sex life. (Amy's mom, Dr. Susanna Braff, is a psychotherapist, so Amy's picked up a lot of the lingo.) I think that's all nonsense, but maybe she's right about my *wanting to get with* the guy at the game today—I'm a lot more enthusiastic than I expected as we spend the next hour sprawled out on her puffy Papasan chair poring over EFM's yearbook. It's also so refreshing to have something besides college apps and premed programs to think about for a change.

Like I was beginning to tell Mr. Blue Eyes before we were so rudely interrupted by Mrs. Ass Crack, I attend Shorr Academy, a K–12 private school that's so small we don't even have a football field. Amy went there for middle school, but after eighth grade she transferred to EFM because she craved

11

its massive art studio, lack of uniform requirement, and hundreds of new guys. I seriously considered following her to public school, but my mom teaches algebra at Shorr, and my parents didn't want me to pass up the free tuition for faculty kids. I also wasn't eager to give up Science Quiz, which is like varsity level *Jeopardy!,* and EFM doesn't have its own team.

As we search through the yearbook, Amy's having a ball pointing out all the guys she's hooked up with, all the guys she hopes to hook up with, and all the guys she thinks I should hook up with. I'm interested in just one guy in particular, and my heart lurches when I spot him among the Gs. Even in black and white, his intense blue eyes seem to leap off the page.

"Bingo!" I shout. I yank the book away from Amy, hold it up close to my face, and pronounce his name. "Wesley Gershwin."

"Really?" Amy leans in and gawks at the photo in amazement. "Gersh was the dude?"

"Uh-oh, is he on your wish list?"

"Oh please, he's way too lanky for me. Don't you remember him from my meets last season?"

I study the headshot for a moment. "Wait, was he a sprinter?"

"Only the best one on the team. In fact," Amy teases as she elbows me in the rib cage, "I bet he'd look *more* familiar if you actually *watched* the events and didn't just do your homework in the stands, best friend."

"Yeah, yeah. So why'd you sound so surprised he's the guy?"

"Well, Gersh is a puzzling breed," she says, stroking her

chin like a mad professor type. "He's cute, smart, well liked, but very shy. He transferred to EFM just last year, and he still has that 'little orphan chipmunk lost in the woods' feel to him, so the fact that he even came up to you and started talking says *a lot*. Oh, Dom!" Amy looks at me, awestruck. "He must have been really drawn to you to come out of his shell like that and offer you Band-Aids!"

"I think you're jumping the gun here. It was a damsel in distress situation, so he was just being chivalrous."

"Exactly. Guys love being the knight in shining armor." Amy takes my cell phone out of my purse and flips it open. "Since you were the one who ran off, you gotta make the next move. Go on, damsel." She poises her forefinger over the keypad. "You know you want to call him. I'll get his number."

"What are you talking about?" I reach over and flip the cell shut. "No way am I going to *call* him! He probably thinks I'm a total dorkus, and that's assuming he even re-members who I am." I settle back into the comfiness of the chair. "The most I'd consider doing is e-mailing. It's a lot less confrontational."

"Ugh. That's so wussy," Amy groans as she flops back next to me. "What if he thinks you're spam and deletes it?"

"It's worth the risk. What I'm *not* willing to risk is being tongue-tied on the phone with a shy boy I'm not even sure I like yet." I grin, satisfied with my pragmatism. Then I catch sight of the time on my cell. "Shit! I need to run to my bratsitting gig."

"One sec." She wriggles off the chair. "Let me dig up the student directory before we forget."

While Amy's searching through her desk drawers, I

resume examining Wesley's handsome face. What a contrast to the sea of goofy, unflattering headshots surrounding his. I turn to the varsity sports section and find a shot of Wesley breaking a finish line ribbon. He looks really sexy with his sweat-saturated nylon EFM singlet clinging to his pecs and abs. I love his arms. They're very thin, but toned. I wonder how much he can bench? I'm a hundred and fifteen pounds—I bet he could bench me. I don't know why I'm even thinking this. I rub my temples.

"And FYI," Amy says as she slaps the directory onto my lap. "Word on the asphalt is Gersh doesn't have a girlfriend."

3

Subject: Hey, we sorta met at the game today. . . .
Date: Wednesday, December 26, 6:45 p.m.

Dear Wesley (a.k.a. Good Samaritan),

Hi. My name is Dominique Baylor, Amy Braff's best friend from Shorr Academy. Amy helped me figure out who you are and gave me your e-mail address so I could write and thank you for pulling me from the mud today and offering to get me Band-Aids. I'm sorry for leaving you alone with that lady, but I was pretty out of it after my tumble and wasn't feeling well. Anyway, I've regained sanity and am perfectly fine now, and I just wanted you to know how much I appreciated your help.

I hope you had a good time at the game otherwise and that you have a great rest of your winter break.

Gratefully and klutzily, Dom

P.S. Merry Belated Christmas!

I press SEND and feel an enormous sense of relief now that I've redeemed myself somewhat. But suddenly I'm scared Wesley's going to think I'm some kind of stalker for tracking him down and e-mailing him. I stare at the computer screen in a mild panic, but then I remember what Amy said before I left her house this afternoon: *What do you have to lose?*

I sigh as I sign off, and then I amble to the dining room, where I see my parents for the first time since Amy picked me up this morning. Even from the kitchen my mom notices my bruised knees right away. "Oh, Dommie, you're hurt!"

"What the hell happened?" my dad booms after throwing down his newspaper. Then he notices I'm still in Amy's gym clothes. "I thought you were going to watch football, not play it."

"Oh yeah, Dad, that's me." I flex my muscles. "EFM MVP."

"Hey, as long as you made the other poor saps look worse." He laughs. "Did you bust some ass out there on the gridiron?" He grinds his fist into the palm of his other hand and grins roguishly.

Mom shoots Dad a cut-it-out look and scurries over to me. "Oh, Dommie, you babysat looking like this? Let me get the Neosporin."

"Mom, I have white blood cells. I'll be fine."

"Let her alone," Dad tells Mom. "I say let her wear her

scars proudly. Check this out." He rolls up his sleeve to reveal a long gash of a scar down his bicep, which he got from a shark-fishing accident twenty years back. Mom ignores him as I pretend to nod appreciatively.

The whole "opposites attract" thing definitely applies to my parents. Mom prides herself on being articulate and orderly, befitting the math teacher she is. Dad, on the other hand, is always swearing and kidding around, which I suppose helps him cope with his job—as the Fort Myers chief of police, Dad has to deal with a lot of heavy stuff.

I know it sounds like juvenile detention, living with a schoolteacher and a police officer, especially since I don't have any siblings to deflect their attention. Luckily they're pretty laid-back in their off hours, and I don't cause them much trouble anyway. Amy bets that Dad brings his handcuffs into bed and that Mom disciplines him with a ruler in kinky role-playing sex games, but I seriously doubt Mom would go for anything that risqué. It's not that I think my parents don't do it anymore. I just figure they keep it really routine and boring, at least compared to the kind of stuff Amy imagines.

Sometimes I'm amazed they're still even attracted to each other after nineteen years of marriage, what with Dad's baldness and stereotypical law enforcement gut and Mom's graying hair and wrinkles (or "wise lines," as she calls them). My parents actually met through a personal ad Dad took out when he was still in the police academy and didn't have much time to meet women. By then Mom had suffered through dozens of bad dates and lost all hope of finding a man she could love. She reluctantly answered the ad on a dare from a fellow teacher and, amazingly, she knew on their first date Dad was her one and only.

Since then very little has changed about them. We still live in the same sixth-floor, two-bedroom apartment they moved into as newlyweds, and we still drive the same station wagon they bought two years later when I was born (though just about every part has since been replaced at least twice). Although Mom and Dad bring in decent salaries, we purposely live below our means so they can put a lot of it toward my college fund. I'm glad my parents found each other, but I'm always embarrassed when people ask how they got together. Using personal ads just seems sketchy and desperate. I hope to meet the love of my life in a more fateful and romantic way.

After dinner my parents time me as I play a few solo rounds of Operation. I realize I'm the only human past age eight who still owns this game, but my human anatomy teacher says that playing Operation or even Pick Up Stix under time pressure is a great way to develop the fine motor skills necessary for performing surgery. I'm not sure I want to be a surgeon yet, but it can't hurt to practice. Tonight on my seventh try I pluck out all thirteen pieces in only twenty seconds, a new record for me. My parents applaud and cheer, which is sweet but makes me feel like a baby.

Soon the three of us migrate to the living room, where Mom and Dad cuddle on the love seat to peruse *Fishing World* magazine, and I channel surf on the couch until I find *The Princess Bride,* one of my favorite movies, which I can watch again and again. I must have been exhausted, though, because next thing I know I'm waking up groggy and confused on the couch. The lights are off, the remote control has fallen onto the floor, and the DVD player is flashing 12:42 a.m. in bright green numbers. When I stand up I feel my knees sting. Then I remember. I stagger as fast as I can to my computer and log on to my e-mail.

Subject: Re: Hey, we sorta met at the game today. . . .
Date: Wednesday, December 26, 10:28 p.m.
Hi Dominique—

You say you're Braff's friend? You must be the redhead I remember seeing hanging around her at our track meets last season. You sit in the back left on the bleachers, right? I wondered who you were.

Glad to hear you weren't hurt too badly. Saw you made it to the bathroom. (It's okay. I have a small bladder too.) I'm serious about what I said about you running track. You were really booking it. Btw, that lady was strange! After you left she said she was the quarterback's mom and started going on about his knee injury, so to get away I pretended I needed to go to the bathroom myself.

My buddy Paul from track (also the wide receiver in the game today) is throwing a New Year's shindig Monday. He just sent the e-vite, so I'll forward it on. Braff's already on the list. Hope to see you there, Dom. With any luck I'll have my college crapplications finished by then. They are such a pain.

—Wes

I lean back in my chair and smile giddily. His e-mail doesn't come right out and say "I like you," but it definitely hints at "more than just-friends" potential.

Or does it?

I log on to AOL Instant Messenger and luckily Amy's still awake. We know each other so well I could have predicted her response.

EFMBabe: Wait. Let me get this straight. Gersh wrote, "It's okay. I have a small bladder too."?!?! Bladder, Dominique, *bladder*!!! Clearly, he was subconsciously thinking about his dick when he wrote you.

DominiqueBaylor: LOL. I think that may be a little far-fetched. The truth is he didn't ask me out. Nothing he said was really flirty. He didn't even give me his cell number or IM screen name.

EFMBabe: No, but he invited you to a party, and he called you by your nickname, Dom, which shows he's already comfortable with you. And he explicitly wrote he "wondered" who you were and "hopes" to see you at the party. Trust me, he wants on.

DominiqueBaylor: You know, I'm going to have a lot of free time this semester since I'll be taking only four classes. It might be fun to pursue one little classic high school sweetheart experience before graduation.

EFMBabe: "Sweetheart experience?" <barfing noises> Just promise you'll never call yourselves Wominique or Desley.

DominiqueBaylor: Shut up! You know what I mean. But now that you mention it, Wesley is a nice name, isn't it? Sounds like Westley from *The Princess Bride*. Very heroic.

EFMBabe: Well, Buttercup, sounds like this semester's gonna be *a lot* more interesting than I thought!

It takes me forty minutes, three spell checks, two Diet Cokes, and a mental debate over whether writing an e-mail in the middle of the night makes me seem like an overeager loser, to come up with what I think could be a final draft.

Good early morning, Wes—

Yes, I did root for Amy at many of her meets last spring, so it's very likely I'm the red-haired girl you remember seeing. And no, I've never thought about running track, but that's mainly because Shorr doesn't have a team.

Good luck finishing your "crapplications"! Where'd you end up applying? My dream school is Stanford, Tulane's my second choice, and University of Florida's my safety. They all have good premed programs, so I'll be happy at any of them. I can't believe we have to wait until April for our acceptances, though. Anyway, thanks for the New Year's invite. Amy and I will be there. Off to bed now, Dom

P.S. FYI, my AIM name is DominiqueBaylor.

Sometime during my fifteenth proofread it hits me that I'm acting ridiculous. I should know better than to waste precious time dissecting some guy's two-kilobyte e-mail for hidden romantic meaning, not to mention staying up until half past one to craft a response. At any rate, in the unlikely event he is interested in me, there's no point in starting anything now since we're probably heading to different colleges in different cities.

As I place the mouse over the DELETE button, I remind myself how in the grand scheme of things he's just a boy, nothing to lose my head over.

So why can't my heart stop racing?

And why do I like how that feels?

I drag the mouse left, breathe deeply, and click SEND.

4

Wes is the first thing that pops into my head when I wake up the next day. I don't remember ever thinking about Matt first thing in the morning, and I've liked him for seven years. Usually all that's on my mind when I wake up is how I need to pee and get ready for Science Quiz practice at Shorr.

This morning, though, I don't need to pee, and I don't have Science Quiz practice until winter break ends next week. I turn to my clock. 10:20. It's so good to sleep in, especially on a Thursday.

I lie in bed for a while, half-asleep, remembering the way Wes looked when he rescued me from the mud. Those blue eyes. The gold sun streaming behind him. The silhouette of his strong, steady arm reaching down just for me.

"Mmmm, Wes," I say under my breath, kind of jokingly. But it does turn me on a little.

Without really thinking about it, I start lightly stroking my breasts with my fingertips until I feel my nipples harden. Then I move my hand down my torso and slowly tickle the area below my belly button. It's so relaxing, but energizing too. I can even feel my undies start to get wet.

I wonder how it would feel if today I go even lower. Sure, I've been curious and touched myself there before, but nothing ever happened. Amy's appalled I've never had a "Big O," as she calls it, but, I don't know . . . I guess I've always been too preoccupied preparing for the next four years of my academic life to have time to care about four seconds of physical pleasure. Suddenly, though, I really want to know what having one is like. In my human anatomy class we learned the clitoris has eight thousand nerve fibers, at least twice as many as a penis. That deserves a little experimentation, and it would be so easy just to walk my fingers a little lower—

Bang bang bang!

I jump, yanking my hand out from under the covers. "Dad?" I blurt out, my heart pounding in my ears. "Don't come in!"

"Why? What's wrong?" he asks from the other side of my unlocked bedroom door. "You have a guy in there with you?"

"Oh yeah, Dad, and I'm hiding him in the closet. One sec."

I tear out of bed, throw on my white terry cloth robe,

and study myself in my full-length mirror. I decide I don't look like I've just tried to masturbate, and I open the door.

After we hug good morning, Dad takes a seat on the foot of my bed and says there's been a change in plans.

"I have to go in to the station this weekend for New Year's prep crap, which means we won't be able to visit Grandma on Sunday. So I'm taking off work so we can go today."

"Dad," I moan, "can't we just skip it this week?"

"You know it's important to your mother that we see Grandma regularly." He playfully punches my shoulder and stands up to leave. "Meet us downstairs when you're ready, and don't forget your sunblock. We're going fishing afterward."

I try to push all thoughts of clitorises, penises, and Wes out of my head as I throw on my clothes and arrange my tackle box, but my heart is still racing when I meet my parents in the garage ten minutes later.

I used to be really close to my mom's parents, and I'd always look forward to our Sunday brunches at their Sanibel bungalow. My grandpa's death when I was eleven hit my grandma really hard, however, and she turned into one of those cantankerous, nagging old ladies I thought existed only on sitcoms. I kept hoping it was just a phase, especially since I had no other grandparents left, but she just keeps getting crankier. Today I'm not even finished pouring Grandma her decaf before she starts laying into me.

"Dominique, stand up straight!"

"Yes, Grandma."

"Oh, your eyebrows are so bushy! They detract from the

green in your eyes." Then she turns to Mom. "Why don't you buy her tweezers?"

Mom answers calmly, "Dommie's eyebrows suit her face well."

"Dom's a beautiful girl," Dad chimes.

"A woman's eyebrows are the archways to her soul," Grandma proclaims, batting her fake eyelashes. "Neglected eyebrows signify a neglected soul."

Suddenly I'm scared Wes thought they were too bushy.

By the time we finish our eggs, I'm accused of being a bad granddaughter for not phoning enough (I still give a courtesy call at least twice a week), and Dad's accused of being a bad son-in-law for not making enough money to allow Mom to stay home (Mom enjoys teaching, and Dad already covers most of Grandma's expenses so *Grandma* doesn't have to work). Mom defends us both, of course, with her special way of sounding firm but noncombative. All in all, nothing's changed in six years.

Weather permitting, Mom, Dad, and I go out on our fishing boat after every trip to Grandma's as a way to overwrite the previous stressful few hours. Both my parents grew up going fishing with their fathers, and it's always been our favorite family activity. I also credit these outings as one of the reasons I got into biology and am so good at dissections—ever since I can remember, I've been using an assortment of tools to unhook, debone, and disembowel our catches before filleting them for dinner.

It was actually because of a frog dissection that Amy and I became best friends. Back in sixth grade we were paired up as lab partners, and Amy was so grossed out by the sight of intestines and smell of formaldehyde that she actually passed out. I felt bad for her and offered to take care of the whole operation in exchange for her writing up the lab report, and she was so grateful she painted this gorgeous picture of a frog on a lily pad for our cover and did all these professional-looking charts and diagrams on her computer. I'm sure it was her visuals that got us the highest grade in the class. After that we started hanging out all the time, and I'm still closer to her than any of my Shorr friends. Amy will sometimes accompany us on the boat, but she's too squeamish even to handle live bait. That she won't touch a shrimp with her hands but will take a random boy's dick into her mouth has always seemed bizarre to me.

Today Dad steers the boat toward Captiva, and we cast our rods in Foster Bay. There're no clouds, and the low line of sand and palm trees around us has a comforting, cradling effect. As I lean against the rail waiting for a tug on my line, I gaze down at the water. It's a shimmering light blue, just like Wes's eyes. I imagine him standing behind me on the boat and holding me steady as I reel in a catfish. Oh no! I forgot to check my e-mail this morning!

I drop the rod at my feet, rummage through my backpack for my cell phone, and try to check my e-mail on it, but of course I can't get a signal.

"Watch it!" Dad shouts as he picks up the rod. "Expensive equipment like this doesn't grow on trees."

"Sorry, Dad. I wasn't thinking."

I shake my head and survey the horizon in an attempt to clear my mind. But within the minute, I imagine Wes and I are walking on a secluded beach somewhere. He tries to take my hand, and I playfully scurry away, knowing there is no chance I could ever outrun the prize-winning sprinter of the EFM track team. He catches up with me a few seconds later and pulls down my bathing suit, causing us both to fall to the sand. . . . I can't believe I'm thinking this stuff when my parents are two feet away.

Five hours of raunchy daydreams later we finally arrive home and I get online first thing, just to be disappointed by an empty in-box. It's only been a day, though, and we're going to see each other Monday at the New Year's party as it is. I console myself with this thought until Instant Messenger's "invitation to chat" window suddenly appears. I don't recognize the screen name, but I have a pretty good hunch. I'm grinning as I accept the hail.

The100MeterDash: Hey Dom. It's Wes Gershwin.

DominiqueBaylor: Oh, hi! Thanks for adding me. How are you?

The100MeterDash: Good. Thought I'd take a break from my essays and make sure your knees were on the mend.

DominiqueBaylor: I'm so glad you did. ☺ Yes, everything's healing nicely. So I know I asked you this over e-mail, but where are you "crapplying"? And what do you think you'll major in?

The100MeterDash: NYU and Fordham. English, definitely. I read a lot.

DominiqueBaylor: Cool! I take it those schools have track teams too?

The100MeterDash: Yep. My parents are also making me apply to Miami since my brother, Arthur, is a sophomore there, but I really want to live in New York City.

DominiqueBaylor: I've never been to NY but always wanted to visit. But enough college talk, I'm sure you're sick of it. How is your day going otherwise? And should I call you Gersh or Wes?

The100MeterDash: Wes. Only trackies call me Gersh. Day's going great. Arthur's here on break, so we're hanging out. Soon I'll take a run with Jessica.

DominiqueBaylor: Who's Jessica? An EFM friend?

The100MeterDash: No, my collie.

DominiqueBaylor: Oh, Jessica's a very human name for a dog.

The100MeterDash: Well, we got her 10 years ago back when we lived in San Antonio. The girl next door, Jessica Sky, had this red-orange hair that matched the collie's fur exactly, so I named it after her.

DominiqueBaylor: She must have been flattered.

The100MeterDash: Well, I don't think she was super thrilled a dog reminded me of her, but we stayed friends, so it's all good. How's your day?

DominiqueBaylor: Good. Went fishing! Must have caught at least 12 bass, and Mom's making 3 of them for dinner. Yum!

The100MeterDash: Bass, eh? That sounds good. I became a vegetarian last year, though, so I can't enjoy that stuff.

DominiqueBaylor: A vegetarian? Uh-oh, you must think I'm some ruthless fish-killer!

This chat lasts over an hour, and Wes hails me the next four nights also! Fortunately, he never says anything assholeish, and I manage to avoid making a fool of myself. I'm also the one who ends all the chats, which is good—Amy always says you're supposed to leave boys wanting more. To my relief Wes never mentions Jessica Sky, or any other girl, again.

The one discouraging aspect of all this IM-ing is Wes never sounds overtly flirty. Mostly we talk about school, movies, and all the cities he's lived in—his Dad's civil engineering firm moved his family five times in the last fifteen years! Amy says Wes's timidity is probably a direct result of his never being able to get settled in any one place, and she suggests I take the lead and start inserting provocative lines like, "Can you hold on, Wes? I have to take my panties out of the dryer." First off, IM-ing about underwear is not my idea of a come-on. But even if it were, I don't want to risk losing this great thing we have going by pressing the issue too early and scaring him away.

The night before the party, however, the tide shifts slightly when he writes:

The100MeterDash: You know, Dom, chatting with you is quickly becoming one of the highlights of my day. G'night.

After rereading the line a few times to make sure I'm not imagining things, I'm unable to form a coherent sentence, so I respond with:

DominiqueBaylor: ☺ ☺ ☺ See ya tomorrow.

If I were gutsier, I'd have written back that chatting with him has become *the* highlight of my day.

5

I dedicate the entire afternoon of New Year's Eve to preparing for the party. In the shower I loofah my feet, knees, and elbows, and I shave my legs, underarms, and bikini area. I even clean out my belly button with a Q-tip. My carefully planned outfit of dark blue hip-hugger jeans and a green wraparound top won't reveal any of those zones, and I certainly won't be taking off any clothes tonight, but it's fun to *feel* ready for anything.

Amy arrives at my place after dinner armed with Revlon's entire cosmetics counter. She's an expert makeup artist, which makes sense since it's a lot like painting. She even plucks my eyebrows for the first time, and I have to admit Grandma was right about it playing up my eyes.

After she's done with my nails and hair, I do a bunch of 360s in front of my full-length mirror and study my posture from all angles.

"You look great," Amy reassures me while bouncing impatiently on my bed. "And you know I'm not just saying that."

"I'm really starting to get nervous, though. What if we just don't click?"

"Well, you've got the double-clicking down. Just try not to barf when you see him this time."

"Ha ha," I drone as I grab my purse. "Let's go."

The closest parking spot we can find to the party is six blocks away. Amy's been to Paul's before, so after I check myself in the passenger side visor mirror for the twelfth time, I follow her as we make our way up the street and then down a weather-beaten wood stairwell leading to the beach.

Paul's parents' beach house—mansion, really—is white, modern, and gorgeous. It's lit up like a birthday cake, with strings of Christmas lights suspended from the roof and tiki torches lining the porches. Halfway between the front porch and the shoreline, a huge bonfire casts patches of gold onto the beach, revealing dozens of guests talking, drinking, eating, and making out on blankets.

Please, Wes, don't be one of the people making out.

As we approach the beach house, I recognize a few old friends who used to attend Shorr, but I'm too intent on finding Wes to concentrate on anyone else. After a couple minutes Amy spots him bent over the mammoth stereo on the patio. We walk toward him.

31

"Nice ass, Gersh," Amy yells over the music. I elbow her in the side.

Wes jumps up and turns around. He's blushing, but it doesn't detract from how manly his loose blue jeans and charcoal gray polo make him look. It's thrilling being this close to him again, but I can feel my throat tighten I'm so nervous.

Wes looks at me first. "Hi, nice to see you again." Then he turns to Amy. "Braff, what's this crap I hear about you dropping out of track?"

"It's not crap," Amy says proudly. "It's my last year, and I want an easy spring."

He shakes his head. "Slacker."

"And proud of it! This semester I'm all about cruising and boozing. Speaking of which," Amy says as she hoists up the shopping bag she's carrying, "we beareth champagne, 'borrowed' from my stepdad's cellar especially for tonight's festivities."

"Cool, can you put it in the fridge?"

"With pleasure!" She grins at me pointedly before leaving.

"And what are these?" Wes asks, stepping closer to me and looking down at the tray I'm carrying. I can feel the sweat drip down my armpits.

"I made chocolate-dipped strawberries."

"Really?" he exclaims, wide-eyed. "Are these all for me?"

I like his voice. It's masculine, but not too deep.

"Well, they're for everybody. But I remember we were, um, IM-ing about our favorite foods, and you said strawberries were yours."

As I watch him devour two of them, my stomach gets that same satiny sensation I used to feel while swinging in the playground.

"Mmm," he says, wiping off some strawberry dribble from his very cute cleft chin. "That was so good."

"I'm glad you like them. . . . Um, do you deejay all the parties you go to?"

"Well, I hate small talk. But if I put myself in charge of something, like the stereo, then I can do that and not worry about making conversation."

"I totally know what you mean. I can't stand small talk either."

I grin at him. He grins at me. Then . . . nothing. Awkward silence alert! He's looking at me anxiously.

I force a smile. "Um, I guess it would help if we liked small talk, huh?"

"Yeah, I guess." He grins back.

Suddenly some guy yells from the living room, "Hey, Gersh, come on! We're playing Grand Theft Auto!"

Wes looks at me sheepishly, and I say, "Go ahead. Kick ass. Here, take the strawberries and share them."

Our fingers brush when I hand him the tray.

"Thanks, Dom. I'll catch you after."

"Yeah. Sure."

So much for my being one of the highlights of his day. A minute later I peer in through the living room's panoramic window and watch as the boys dive into my strawberries and their virtual world. I once read in a teen magazine that guys think about sex almost constantly. If that's true, how come we girls get upstaged by sports and video games?

I retreat to the kitchen to look for Amy, but, not to my surprise, I find her on the pool table making out with one of her designated hookups from her art history class. So I spend the remaining two hours of the year on the patio, pretending to join the boring conversation of some girls Amy and I knew from middle school. They devote fifteen minutes to the topic of perfume alone. At one point we dance in a circle to the music, but the juvenility of it all makes me feel pathetic. All the while I keep an eye on Wes through the window. He never takes his eyes off the TV screen, and I start wondering what I'm even doing here.

At about five to midnight, everyone descends upon the living room, where the boys reluctantly shut off their game and switch to MTV so we can watch the ball drop in Times Square.

Several couples start embracing, and for a moment I lose sight of Wes in the crowd. I sense someone come up behind me. I freeze. Then that someone gently tugs my hair. I spin around . . . it's just Amy.

We watch as Wes and his friends toast with their beer mugs and chug. I know Amy has already told me she thinks he's single, but it's still a relief to see he doesn't kiss anyone at midnight.

Once the ruckus subsides, Amy whispers to me, "Carpe diem."

I take a few deep breaths as we approach my prey. Hope wells up inside of me again.

Wes turns to us and says, "Heya, Braff. Dom, this is Paul."

"Hey, Paul!" I chirrup as we shake hands. "Great job on

the game the other day!" It's like my voice has gone into hyperoverdrive and I've lost the ability to sound chill. I press my lips together.

"Thanks," Paul says indifferently.

Awkward silence. Again.

"So," Amy addresses Paul, "I heard they renovated EFM's library over break. Have you seen it yet?"

"No, but it's supposed to be sweet. All-new computers with voice recognition software and . . ."

While Amy and Paul jabber on, Wes and I stand there listening, occasionally exchanging glances and half smiles. I notice a tiny scar on Wes's right cheek, right below his eye, and his two front teeth overlap ever so slightly. It's really adorable. But then he says he needs to get going.

"Oh," I finally speak up, "but it's barely after midnight."

"I've been here since seven, and I'm sure Jessica needs a bathroom break by now."

"Can't your parents take her out?" I ask.

"They're at a party in Naples and won't be back till late."

"Actually," Amy interjects, "Dom and I should probably get going too. But *I'm* gonna hit the bathroom first. Dom, can *you* go start up the car and turn on the heat?"

"Sure thing, Ames," I say as she hands me the keys.

Wes then offers to walk me to the car, like I know Amy was hoping he would.

Before heading to the bathroom, Amy addresses me with a wily expression. "Remember, make sure to *turn on the heat*!"

6

"**B**rrr." I shiver as we step onto the patio. "It's nippy out, isn't it?"

Nippy? Nippy? Why can't I just shut up?

"Nah," he broods, "it's nothing compared to New York. . . . Watching Times Square on TV just now got me nostalgic for it."

"But you never lived there?"

"No, but my grandparents live in SoHo. We visit them a lot, so it feels like home."

"I see. If—I mean, *when*—you get into NYU or Fordham, are you going to run the marathon?"

"Yeah, but I'll probably come in last. I'm bad at distance."

"Well, just the fact you're even willing to try to run twenty-six miles nonstop is pretty ambitious."

"You want to go to med school. *That's* ambitious."

"Well, thanks." I smile at him.

Wes says a few more goodbyes as we walk the small stretch of beach back toward the stairwell leading to the street. The night gets really quiet as we leave the din of the party behind us. We're in a fancy neighborhood, where tall majestic palms and high white stucco walls surround each home. I wonder what kind of house Wes lives in, and what his room is like.

"So, did you win at Grand Theft Auto?"

"We didn't finish the game. I, um, I wasn't expecting to play for so long, Dom. It's just so addictive."

"I understand. I was never allowed to have Nintendo or anything like that, but I used to play at Amy's. It's fun."

"Yeah, but that stuff's a big time and money sucker. I don't blame your parents for sparing you. As you could probably tell, Paul's parents aren't home much."

"Yeah. My parents are home *too* much."

We both laugh, but soon the only noises are our breathing and our footsteps on the stone sidewalk.

"So, what did you do today?" I ask finally.

"Ran, read, helped my dad take down the tree. You?"

I'm not about to admit I spent half of it preparing to see him.

"Um, I bratsat a neighbor's kid. Then I was gearing up for Science Quiz. You know, our team won the state championship the last three years. We're hoping to go for four."

"Mmm," he hums, looking at the ground.

I'm convinced I'm boring him. Heck, I'm boring myself.

How can we keep a conversation going online for an hour but have nothing to say in person?

We're silent for the last block and a half. When we arrive at Amy's Camry, he takes the keys from my hand and opens the passenger side door for me. I just can't end the night having made so little progress.

I muster my courage. "Thanks, Wes. . . . Um, do you want to keep me company?"

"Um, sure."

As soon as he takes his place behind the wheel, the overhead lights fade out. I can tell his breathing has gotten faster in the last few seconds. So has mine. Fast breathing can be a physiological reaction to sexual arousal. If I were like Amy, I'd be jumping him right about now. Instead, I go in for the kill with another riveting question.

"So, what kind of car do you drive?"

"A Ford Explorer."

"Nice!"

"Nice for having a hundred thousand miles. It used to be my brother's back when he was in high school. There're tons of burn marks on the upholstery from his cigarette mishaps."

"Hey, I'm jealous you have a car at all. I just have a road bike, which works out okay unless the weather is bad or if I want to wear something nice. I have to hitch rides a lot."

"That's another thing I like about New York City. You can walk everywhere."

Amy arrives a few seconds later. I feign nonchalance in telling Wes I'll be on IM tomorrow night. He grins and says I should drop by their first meet next week to root for the team.

"Yeah." I smile back. "I'll be there."

"Cool. The strawberries were wicked dee-lish, by the way."

"I'm glad." I smile wider.

"And I guess I *won't* be seeing you at practice Wednesday, expatriate," Wes pesters Amy as they switch places.

"You can count on it, Gersh. . . . Hey, Dom, you didn't turn on the heat!"

Wes says, "Oh, sorry." He holds out his hand. "Dom didn't get the chance. I have the keys."

Amy starts putting me through the third degree before we even turn the corner. After recounting everything I remember, I end with, "Sitting next to him just now was so—" I can't think of the right word. "Ames, I don't know how this is happening so quickly, but I think I could really, really like him."

"Wow." Amy turns to me, her eyes solicitous. "Even though things were kind of awkward tonight?"

"Yeah, I just know there's chemistry there. . . . I also kind of like that Wes is on the quiet side. It probably means he's deep."

"Well, this is all uncharted territory for me. I don't think I've met a guy yet I liked *that* much, as more than just a hookup."

"It's kind of nice." I pause and look out the window. Just a few minutes into a new year and already so much possibility. "A little frustrating, but nice."

7

Subject: Food!
Date: Wednesday, January 16, 12:14 a.m.

Hey Dom,

This Sunday my parents are having the trackies over to our place. We're probably gonna order up Chinese and watch some of the James Bond marathon on Spike TV. It'd be great if you could come too. Even though she jilted the team, feel free to invite Braff so there'll be someone else there you'll know.—Wes

If you can believe it, this is the fifteenth e-mail Wes has sent me since New Year's! It's also the shortest. He usually writes upward of eight to ten paragraphs, and the subjects run the gamut from *Family Guy* (his favorite TV show) to how the only thing he hates about being vegetarian is the nasty protein shakes his coach makes him drink. Even though the tone of what he writes is still platonic, I've convinced myself that flirtation is better measured by quantity than quality.

Wes and I have been sticking to e-mailing because we haven't been able to find common time to IM like we did before New Year's—track practice keeps Wes from getting home until eight or nine some nights, and I have to go to bed super early to make seven a.m. Science Quiz practice. I don't mind, though. There's something special about corresponding with lengthy e-mails the way people used to with snail mail.

On Sunday I arrive at Wes's fifty minutes late and in a bad mood because Grandma was particularly unpleasant during brunch this morning, my bike is in the repair shop, and Mom, who promised to drive me, was held up at an emergency faculty meeting. On top of everything, Dad was rummaging through our fridge this afternoon for a beer and accidentally toppled the tray of chocolate-dipped strawberries I made especially for tonight.

When I ring Wes's doorbell, a tall blond lady in a pink sweatsuit answers.

"Oh, look at that red hair! You must be Dominique! I'm Wesley's mom." She takes my hand in both of hers. "Wesley has said wonderful things about you."

"Oh . . . that's nice of him," I say, honestly a little shocked. Talking to his mom about me has got to be a good sign. It's funny—his mom, with her big hair and pastel

41

clothes, is so old-school Florida Fabulous while Wes is so understated. But I can see where Wes gets his sharp nose and cleft chin from.

Mrs. Gershwin leads me to the den, where Mr. Gershwin is hunched over some papers at his desk. He's also wearing a sweatsuit, this one in green and yellow. There's no resemblance to Wes in his apple-shaped face and dark brown hair, but he does have those big blue eyes. Mr. Gershwin stands up to shake my hand and says he's glad Wes has made a "good friend" and I should sit next to them from now on during meets. I'm positively beaming!

Mr. and Mrs. Gershwin are on the old side, probably eight to ten years older than my parents, but they're smiley and vivacious and ask me all about Shorr and premed programs. I'm almost disappointed to leave them when Amy appears at the den door and motions for me to come with her. After I say my goodbyes and thank-you-for-having-me-overs, I join Amy in the guest bathroom, which is decked out with jungle-print wallpaper and a gold papier-mâché parrot dangling from the ceiling.

"So," she whispers, "you're fashionably late."

"Yeah, I know. I should have just asked you to pick me up. You all weren't waiting for me to watch the movies, were you?"

"No, but . . ." She leans in close to me, her wavy black hair cresting over her shoulders as she bounces up and down excitedly. "Gersh asked me where you were, like, *three* times."

My blood's pounding in my ears. "Oh my God, really?" I whisper-shout to her.

"Yeah! He kept saying, 'So where's Dom? Shouldn't she be here by now?'"

"Oh, Ames." It's hard to talk I'm smiling so widely. "You know, at the meet yesterday, he was walking to the sidelines to get some water, and he spotted me on the bleachers. He gave me the cutest smile and winked. Winking is much sexier than waving, right?"

"Coming from Gersh, that's like a dozen roses."

"Exactly! I think something could happen tonight if we could finally get some alone time. I know it's only been three weeks—"

"Only three weeks? My patience runs out after three minutes." Amy looks pensive for a moment, the way she does when she's holding her palette before a blank canvas. Finally she says, "All right, I figured it out. There's a guy here I wouldn't mind hooking up with, so if all goes right, we'll both be getting lucky."

"What are you going to do?"

"No questions. Just follow my lead."

We walk into the living room, packed with over twenty trackies spread out on couches, ottomans, armchairs, and the Persian rug. Wes grins bashfully as soon as he sees me.

"Hey, take a seat," he says softly while sidling left to make room between him and Paul on the couch. Meanwhile, Amy heads straight toward one of the discus throwers and seats herself on his lap as if they had been going out for months.

There's a huge spread of Chinese food in front of me on the coffee table, but I'm too wired to eat with there being only an inch of airspace between Wes and me. Soon Wes stretches out his legs so his right ankle ends up resting against my left pinkie toe. It's as if a bolt of electricity surges through me, and all systems are on high alert. I freeze, careful not to move but also unsure of my next move. I try to catch Amy's eye to see if she noticed anything, but she's totally preoccupied with her guy. I already know what she'd advise me to do, anyway.

I take a deep breath and am on the verge of returning a little foot pressure when Wes crosses his legs. My heart sinks into my stomach. Maybe his touching me was completely unintentional after all.

At the end of the evening, after almost everyone else has gone, Amy tells Wes she's bushed and wonders if he could drive me home since I'm so far out of her way. Wes says sure, adding he needs to fill up with gas anyway. I could kiss Amy for being so sympathetic to my cause.

A minute later she walks out with discus boy. Wes and I are left alone, and things are suddenly a little tense. We both know what the two of them are going to do now—it's like they left behind a hookup vibe that Amy, I'm sure, means for me to take advantage of.

"Hey, can you help me straighten up the living room before I drive you?" Wes asks me. "I don't want my mom to wake up and walk in here and go ballistic over the mess."

Great, you're already talking about taking me home.

"Sure! I don't need to get back right away, anyway," I say, trying to sound chipper. I grab an empty takeout carton and start flattening it.

A few minutes later, after we've cleaned the coffee table with the DustBuster and taken out the trash, I pipe up, "So, it was cool to have us all over and order us dinner."

"Yeah . . . I think my parents wish I were more, you

know, social, so they do stuff like this a couple times a semester."

"I'm glad I got to meet them; they were really nice. I like
your house too."

"Well, I can give you the fifty-cent tour if you'd like."

*I'd pay you a lot more than that if your bedroom is on the
tour.* "Yeah, that'd be great."

On the way to the stairwell I trip over the hallway's Persian runner and grunt like an ogre as my knees slam against
the floor. I grab his arm so I don't fall flat on my face.

He laughs. "Traveling by foot isn't exactly your strong
suit, is it?"

"Yeah. I don't know why I've been so clumsy lately,"
I mutter, trying not to sound like I'm going to die of embarrassment. I purposely take my time regaining my
balance, though, releasing his arm at the last possible
second.

From the outside, Wes's house looks like a generic, beige
stucco split-level home, but inside, each room is painted in
a different pastel color, reminding me of Wes's parents'
sweatsuits. There's also a really cozy basement furnished
with leather couches, Chinese lanterns, and even one of
those stereos from the seventies with a turntable and drop-
down spindle. *What a great make-out room,* I think.

Wes's bedroom is on the last leg of our tour. It's boyishly
messy, with a tangle of papers, sneakers, and computer ca-
bles spread out over the powder blue carpet. Posters of
Olympic runners hang above his stuffed bookshelves. Dozens
of track trophies, plaques, and medals sit atop his dresser.
The cutest part—he has Marvin the Martian bedsheets. I

don't know why, but I immediately wonder how many wet dreams he's had on them, and how often he jacks off. I haven't tried touching myself since the time Dad almost walked in on me, although I've thought about it.

"I really like your room," I say, hoping he can't read my mind.

"The best is this." He points to the minifridge and fruit bowl underneath his desk. "I keep various stashes here, like Gatorades and energy bars."

I am expecting him to lead me out of his room and take me home, but instead he breaks off two bananas, throws one to me, and sits down on the floor. So I sit down too, a few feet away from him. After I peel the banana, it occurs to me that eating it normally might resemble performing a blow job. I want to look attractive, not trashy. So I break off bite-sized pieces with my fingers and pop them into my mouth one at a time.

Wes's collie, who's been following us the whole time, bounds onto his lap. I'm not really a pet person, but I figure I better make some kind of nice remark about the animal when I see how it makes Wes's eyes light up.

"Jessica has to be the most darling dog on Earth," I say, trying not to feel jealous as it crawls all over Wes. "You've had her since she was a puppy, right?"

"Yeah. She'll be eleven soon."

"It must have been good to have her with you through all your moves, if you were always making new friends."

"Yeah, she was always there for me. Along with my books and my brother—well, until he went away to college."

"Oh, is this him?" I ask, pointing to a framed photograph on Wes's desk.

"Yep. That's me and Art the Fart in the City. And that's the Washington Square Arch behind us. My grandparents live a few blocks from there."

"He looks like you."

"I think he'd take that as an insult."

I laugh and ask if he has any older family photos. Wes says his mom keeps them in the basement and that he'd be glad to show me. "Just promise not to trip walking down the stairs," he adds, smiling over his shoulder. I'm glad he can joke around with me.

When we get to the basement I pluck an album from the shelf and start leafing through it on the hardwood floor. Wes kneels behind me and leans over my right shoulder so he can see. Somehow I work up the nerve to rock back so my right shoulder blade is ever so slightly resting against his chest.

"That's Mom." He points to a thirty-something blonde in a bikini. I can tell her hair color is natural in the picture, unlike its current shade of platinum.

"She used to be pretty," I blurt out. "I mean, she still is."

"Yeah. Dad picked a fox."

I wonder if he considers me a "fox."

He continues, "Here they are on their honeymoon on Captiva Island. My grandparents, the ones in SoHo, keep a condo on Captiva where they vacation sometimes."

"Cool. My grandparents used to drive to Captiva once a week to eat at The Bubble Room. I don't think Grandma's been back, though, since Grandpa died."

I turn the page and see more honeymoon pictures of Wes's parents, this time with Wes's brother as a two-year-old. Wes can tell I'm perplexed.

He explains, "They had Arthur before they got married. Mom was actually pregnant with me when they made it legal."

"Oh," I say, blushing as I thumb through the next few pages. I've always wondered if my parents had sex before they got married. I wonder if Wes has had sex yet. He's a senior, a jock, and cute, so he's the last person you'd expect to be a virgin. But he's never mentioned having a girlfriend, not that you need to be in a relationship to get laid. I wish I could ask him how far he's gone, but Amy says talking too much about past love lives can get you stuck in friend zone.

I flip to another page and find a picture of young Wes wearing a cone-shaped birthday hat and blowing out eight candles on a race car cake.

"You're so cute! Are all these people your family?"

"No, these are the Skys, our neighbors from San Antonio. There's the original Jessica, see?" Wes points to a pretty red-haired girl, about ten, sitting next to him. She's probably a beauty queen now.

"Oh. So this is the girl next door with the dog-fur hair?"

"Yeah." He chuckles. "Jess is also the one who got me into running. She and my brother would jog every morning, and I'd tag along. Now she runs track at Columbia University."

"Very impressive. Do you guys, um, talk often?"

"Nah."

Phew.

"But our families vacation together every spring break. This year we're meeting in Paris. Jess is a French major, so she wants to practice speaking it."

"Paris? That will be so much fun!" I pretend being excited for him, but I'm crushed he's not going to be in town over break. I also can't help wondering if Jessica is part of the reason he wants to go to college in New York.

As I continue flipping through party pictures, I ask when his birthday is.

"December twenty-second."

"Get out!" I turn my head to his. Our lips are about eight inches apart. "December twenty-second is *my* birthday! But wait, you're probably eighteen, right?"

"Aren't you?"

I shake my head. "Seventeen. They started me early because I was too mature for nursery school."

"They started me late because I was too *im*mature."

After we both laugh, I look back at the album, but all I can concentrate on are Wes's breaths landing on the back of my neck. The heart beats an average of seventy times a minute. Right now mine is doing a hundred and twenty easy, and with each inhalation I'm drinking in Wes's healthy, clean scent—a delicious combination of sweat and fabric softener. In biology we learned how animals can smell each other's pheromones, chemical signals that prompt them to mate. I can almost hear my pheromones bouncing into Wes's.

When we finish the album, Wes gets up to reshelve it. I take the opportunity to move this operation to the couch. He follows me but sits on the opposite side, holding his knees to his chest with his forearms. Not exactly the most receptive pose.

We stare into space for a couple minutes before I say, "Mmm . . . I really like your house. I feel so at home here."

Then out of nowhere Wes grins and makes the most promising statement of the evening. "I'm really happy you were able to come tonight."

I rush in with, "Me too. I had a lot of fun."

Wes shifts his position and leans toward me. My heart starts racing again and I instinctively wet my lips.

Then he stops and says, "I should take you home. I don't want your dad to be mad at me for keeping you out late, him being the chief of police and everything."

"Yeah," I answer, attempting to sound indifferent. "I do have to be up in, like, five hours as it is to make Science Quiz practice."

Wes is mute on the drive to my place, and I can't think of anything not small-talky to say. So I close my eyes and pretend to sleep. When we get to my apartment building, he murmurs, "Dom? Dom?"

I am hoping he'll try to wake me by gently nudging me. Or perhaps by kissing me. The moment is perfect.

Suddenly the car stereo is blasting rap at full volume.

"Okay, I'm up, I'm up! Turn that off!"

"Couldn't resist." He laughs. "See you at the next meet."

I feel as if I'm tied to the passenger seat. There's no way we can part ways this unemotionally after how much we've talked tonight, let alone been e-mailing. I clear my throat, smile, and extend my right arm toward him, inviting him in for a hug. He leans into me for only a couple seconds before pulling back and saying goodbye again.

I bow my head in defeat. "Good night, Wes."

Subject: Have a minute?
Date: Monday, January 21, 1:31 a.m.
Dear Wes,

When I got to my bedroom just now, I thought, *Yes! Finally I'll get some sleep.* I jumped into bed, and then I thought, *Wow, this was such an awesome night.*

So before I hit the hay, I wanted to write and let you know I had mucho fun talking to you just now. I totally enjoy our e-mails, and hanging with your friends tonight was great, but it was triply great just being with you without anyone else around. I really felt like I got to know you better. Maybe we could arrange for something similar again soon, if you want and if you have time.

Anyway, off to bed now. Hugs, Dom

Subject: Yes, I have a minute
Date: Monday, January 21, 2:00 a.m.
I agree. We need to hang out more before the year is up. I wish we'd met before we did. I always wanted to go up into the bleachers and introduce myself to you at the meets last year, but I was afraid you'd think I was strange. I really wish I had now, we could have spent more time together. Dom, I hope we keep in touch after graduation. I'll be really bummed if we don't. G'night.—W

9

Being an only child, I can't help that my parents are really tuned in to my life and can detect when something's on my mind besides school. They finally confront me one evening in late January. When they walk into my room, I turn off my monitor so they won't see I'm in the middle of e-mailing Wes.

Dad sits down on the foot of my bed and asks, "Have you been feeling all right?"

"Yeah, why? Have *you* been feeling all right?" I know I'm sounding adversarial, but I'm *really* ticked off at them for interrupting my train of thought.

"We're a little concerned, Dommie. You seem preoccupied," Mom says.

"Preoccupied?" I guffaw dismissively. "Don't you remember last semester? College crapplications? The SATs? I am perfectly relaxed in comparison."

Mom nods but says, "It's just that lately we barely see you. You hardly touch your dinner, and then you race into your room."

"What are you trying to say?"

"What your father and I are asking you is if you're having any bad thoughts or feelings about eating, or your body."

Normally, I laugh good-naturedly when my parents jump to crazy conclusions. Instead, I roll my eyes and raise my voice.

"Mom, don't be crazy. I do not have an eating disorder."

"Don't call your mother crazy," Dad stays sternly.

"Tonight, for instance," Mom goes on, "you didn't eat the bass Daddy caught, and that's your favorite."

"That's because I've been toying with the idea of becoming a vegetarian."

"A vegetarian!" Dad's already losing his cool. It usually takes a lot longer for that to happen.

"Oh," Mom says thoughtfully. "Well, I guess I could start preparing some more veggies with dinner—"

"Veggies, schmeggies," Dad barks at me. "Having meat in your diet is important!"

I can't believe how out of touch he is. "Dad, you can totally get the benefits of meat from other things, like these energy bars I've been devouring." I open my desk drawer to reveal my new stockpile. "They're made with real tofu."

"Tofu? Tofu is nothing more than white shit. What the hell brought this on? Wait—" Dad sounds like he's having a revelation. "You're not falling for that animal rights propaganda crap, are you? Is this why you haven't been coming fishing with us?"

"Calm down, Dad. Although fishing *is* a pretty cruel sport when you think about it, I'm being vegetarian for purely nutritional reasons, and it's been working." I try to smile pleasantly. "Honestly, I've never felt so energetic before."

After a silence I continue, "Is that all you came in to say?"

"Well," Mom hedges, "we were wondering—"

"Are you talking a lot with that boy?" Dad asks brusquely. "The one whose movie party you went to?"

Finally, they get to the point. After a heavy sigh, I answer proudly, " 'That boy' has a name. It's Wes. Yes, we e-mail once a day, we've hung out a couple times, and I go to his track meets. He's an amazing athlete."

"Since when do you care about sports?" Mom asks.

"And what kind of stinkin' athlete runs around in big circles because he's too sissy to play ball?" Dad whines.

"Whatever. And Mom, I don't have to like sports to appreciate athletic skill. I used to go watch Amy all the time, and you never gave me a hard time about that."

After another silence Mom says, "Certainly, it's normal for girls your age to want . . . friends of the opposite sex—" Dad's grumbling interrupts her. "And your father and I don't want to discourage that." Dad grumbles louder. "It just seems to me you're giving this boy more time than you did your Stanford and Tulane applications."

"Oh my God!" I look at her really meanly. "I worked

months on those essays. I'm so hurt you'd even think that. And Dad." I look straight at him. "I hate it when you interrogate me like I'm some criminal you've arrested."

"We'll leave you alone now." Dad grumbles again while getting up, but I know he is about to read me my rights. "You shouldn't make this boy so important if all he's doing is distracting you. And there's no reason to get so defensive when we try to talk to you about it. As for this vegetable business, never feel bad about eating meat. Human beings have been doing it for millennia, and that's why they thrived. You understand what I'm saying?"

"I appreciate your anthropological assessment, Dad, but I really need to get back to work now."

Dad tries to smile, obviously feeling bad. "Uh . . . wanna play a few rounds of Operation?"

"Maybe later."

I swivel my chair around and wait until my parents close the door to resume my e-mail, but I have trouble getting back into the flow because I'm so steamed at them for questioning my judgment. They don't even know Wes, and I wasn't lying when I said being a vegetarian has improved my health. True, I probably wouldn't have cut out meat had it not been for Wes, but so what? I figure it would be hard for him to think about dating someone he saw as a bloodthirsty carnivore. Amy always says a girl should never change herself to please a boy, but Wes has never asked me to change. Part of knowing cool people is adopting their best attributes. Besides, I don't think changing for someone is bad as long as you're objectively changing for the better.

10

It's the second week of February, and Wes is finally coming to a Science Quiz match. I had second thoughts about asking him because I know his being there will make me nervous. But after six weeks of watching from the bleachers as Wes outruns every other senior in central Florida, I'm anxious to reverse roles and have him see me be the center of attention.

Tonight Wes will also finally meet my parents, who have been on my case about never asking him over. Amy wisely suggested that having introductions take place at Shorr rather than our apartment would prevent my parents from bringing up embarrassing stories and grilling him with questions.

Best of all, after the match Wes and I are going over to his house. It'll be the third time we've hung out there since his movie party, except now his parents are in Miami visiting his brother, so we'll have the entire place to ourselves! I've been popping breath mints all day in anticipation of our inevitable first kiss.

Shorr Academy resembles New England private schools in its austere, spartan decor, but the auditorium, a collective gift from some of the rich parents, is really beautiful. The floor is constructed entirely of pink and gray marble, and two Graeco-Roman-style columns flank the entranceway. Red velvet curtains frame the stage, which is where my four teammates and I sit behind a long table while the opposing team, from a school in Fort Lauderdale, is being teleconferenced in on our fifty-two-inch plasma screen.

With Wes in the audience, I feel extra special having a spotlight trained on my face. I'm the only girl on either team, and I think I look kind of sexy in my plaid pleated skirt, white button-down oxford, blue blazer, kneesocks, and high-heeled loafers. I'd rather Wes not see me get any questions wrong, so I don't buzz in unless I'm absolutely sure of the answer.

The last question of the night is "What's the common name for the reproductive organs that produce gametes?" I want to pass on this one too, but the teams are tied and this is the semifinals, so if we lose this, we're out for the season.

After hesitating for a moment, I murmur "gonads" into the mike. Immediately everyone in the audience starts howling. Even the moderator cracks a smile, and I can feel myself blush. But as everyone starts applauding our win, I think maybe it's good Wes heard me say something sex related. After all, I want him to view me as someone sexual. In some weird way, I'm glad my parents heard me too. I'm not their little girl anymore.

After every match, Shorr hosts a minireception in the back of the auditorium complete with the customary cheese-and-crackers buffet table. Normally, I find my parents in their front row seats and we walk together to get punch. Today I give them a quick wave and head straight for Wes, who is standing by the side entrance.

"Hey, stranger." I smile. "I see you found Shorr okay."

"Eventually. Sorry I was late."

"It's okay. A little different from track, huh?"

"Yeah, but just as nerve-racking! If I were up there, I don't know if I could remember my own name, let alone ' 'nads.' "

Oh God, all I want to do is kiss you.

I grin. "Let's find my parents."

They are already walking toward us.

"Congratulations, sweetheart!" Mom kisses me. "Those were some tough questions."

"You made us proud," Dad says during our hug, although he's clearly already checking out Wes.

"Thanks. Um, guys, this is Wesley Gershwin."

After an exchange of handshakes and nice-to-meet-yous and the obligatory what-colleges-are-you-applying-to conversation, Dad says eagerly, "How 'bout we treat you kids to dinner? Wesley, we live right by this great seafood dive. Biggest prawns you ever saw. And lobster tacos."

"Um, Dad, Wes is a vegetarian."

"Oh . . . oh," Dad utters, suddenly understanding.

Wes says, "Thanks for the offer, Mr. Baylor, but I need to get back and feed my dog."

I'm disappointed Wes said "I" and not "we." He was the one who suggested we hang out tonight.

"Yeah," I say to my parents, "and this is one of the few nights Wes doesn't have track practice, so we were just going to kick back with some takeout and a movie."

Dad looks dejected, and Mom takes his hand. "Well, have fun kids. Dommie, how late do you think you'll be?"

"Until whenever the movie ends. See ya!"

My annoyance at Wes's lack of assertiveness quickly fades as I contemplate a whole evening alone with him. It's such a nice change walking through Shorr's parking lot to Wes's Explorer rather than my parents' station wagon.

Three hours later the credits to *The Princess Bride* are rolling on Wes's TV. He's lounging in his desk chair, facing the screen. I'm sitting cross-legged at the foot of his bed. When Wes turns off the TV, the room is pitch black.

"That was great," he exclaims. "I can't believe I've never seen it before."

"Yeah, you've been missing out. It's such a timeless classic." I lie back. Then a pause. "Your bed is so comfortable."

"Yeah, sometimes I try to do homework on it, but I just end up falling asleep."

"I can imagine. I could just lie here for hours." I sigh, the vision of the movie's last kiss lingering in my head.

After a moment Wes turns on the desk lamp, picks up the dog, reaches for a Gatorade, and asks if I want one.

"No thanks," I say disappointedly as I sit up, my eyes stinging from the light. In *The Princess Bride,* Westley falls for Buttercup even though she's a bitch to him. Here I am being all nice and inviting, and nothing! How much more encouragement does this guy need? And I know what's coming when he finishes his last swig.

"Dom, Jessica needs to be walked."

I scowl at the snivelly animal as I pull up my kneesocks and slip on my loafers. But then I ask, referencing a joke from the movie, "Would it be so 'inconceivable' if Jessica skipped one walk?"

I was trying to be funny about it, but Wes looks at me like I'm some fascist dictator. "Dom, it'd be really cruel not to take her out. Why would I do that?"

"Oh. You're totally right. Sorry. Forget it." I'd do anything to erase the last five seconds, but he doesn't seem too pissed as we head downstairs and outside, so I try to relax.

One would think a late-night stroll around the palm-tree-studded neighborhood would be romantic, but within minutes the dog lets loose on the lawn. I realize shitting on the grass is a perfectly natural canine behavior, but the ugly presence of bodily waste is the king of all romantic buzz kills. Whenever I'm over at Wes's, I always opt to use the guest bathroom even though he says it's fine if I use his own. I can't bear the thought of his being in earshot of my pee hitting the toilet water, let alone anything else that might escape.

On the way back to his place, I actually consider faking a fall so Wes could pull me to my feet and we could have some physical contact. I know that's pathetic, and it's not even worth trying, anyway—both his hands are already occupied, one with the leash and one with the plastic bag of shit he scooped up. Soon he picks up the dog itself.

"Last week the vet said she has arthritis, so she needs to take it easy."

Then why are we walking her in the first place?

"Oh no! Poor thing."

When we finally arrive back at his house, Wes lets the dog in and says he'd better drive me home so he can rest up for the meet tomorrow. If I hear the words "meet" or "track" one more time I think I'm going to scream. I'm so aggravated the last thing I want to do before I get out of his car is give him our good night hug, but I do. It's the tightest and longest one so far.

"See you at the meet tomorrow, Dom."

"Yeah. See you tomorrow." I pause. "Hey, Wes?"

"Yeah?"

I like you, Wes. Soooo much. Could you like me that way too? If so, stop giving me mixed signals and kiss me!

"What is it, Dom?"

"Um, you know, sleep well, and knock 'em dead tomorrow."

A month ago it would have been my dream just to be in his bedroom watching a movie, but now it's torture because I want so much more. It's like my entire conscious state has been reduced to this toxic blend of hope and uncertainty. I hate that I have to act cool and almost pretend I don't like him when in fact I do, because, God forbid, I might come across as desperate for affection or a little clingy, which everyone should know are perfectly natural human behaviors, after all. Ugh!

11

Mom has a PTA meeting the last Friday of February, so Dad and I are on our own for dinner. I feel distracted because Wes hasn't e-mailed me in two days, and my hope of ever getting together with him is at an all-time low. I know Wes is busy with his track schedule and he can't always e-mail me back within twenty-four hours, but the fact that he's not even taking the trouble to text me a quick hello is just further proof he's not interested. As if I needed any more proof.

Adding insult to injury, Dad orders up Chinese from the vegetarian place I know Wes likes. The dinner conversation isn't helping my mood, although for once Dad's not his usual loud, swearing self.

"So, Dom, I've been meaning to ask you for a while now, did that Wes boy do anything special for you on Valentine's Day?"

" 'That Wes boy'? It's Wes, Dad." I push the rice around with my fork. "And why would he do something? It's not like we're dating or anything."

After dinner I start writing my English paper on Emily Dickinson, but I keep thinking about what Dad said. Wes didn't even mention Valentine's in his e-mail that day. I was so disappointed. I'm still disappointed.

I try again to concentrate on my paper, but every word I read or write reminds me in some twisted, far-fetched way of Wes. "Parallel structure" makes me think of his perfect coordination as he runs. So does "onomatopoeia." I swear I can hear the whisper of his sneakers slamming into the asphalt every time I speak his name. *Gersh-Win-Gersh-Win-Gersh-Win-Gersh-Win.*

I hold up my right hand and examine my mood ring, which Wes won for me at Skee-Ball when I tagged along with the track team at the arcade last week. Well, technically he didn't win it *for* me. He won it, and then he gave it to me because he didn't want it for himself. However, at least half the track team was there, which included eleven girls, so it must mean something that Wes chose to unload it on me rather than some other girl. The only explanation he gave was "I don't do jewelry."

My writer's block is pretty insurmountable at this point, so I shut down my computer and collapse on my bed. Then I imagine Wes at a meet jumping hurdles and tripping over one of them . . . and tearing a ligament or two . . . and having to drop out of track . . . which would free up his evenings . . . which maybe he'd choose to spend with me. Wes told me he had tripped over a hurdle before, back in tenth grade. That's how he got that little scar under his eye. It's possible he could trip again. Am I evil for having these thoughts?

I consider calling Amy to complain, but then I remember she's on a date, which just makes me feel more like a loser. Anyway, she'd just repeat the advice she's been giving me for the last month: (A) jump him, (B) ask him point-blank what's going on with us, or (C) drop him like a bad habit. I tried to explain to her that I don't want to set myself up for rejection, especially in case Wes isn't sure of his feelings yet, so that rules out *A* and *B*. As for *C*, I can't drop him, I'm in too deep. That's the one thing Amy can't seem to understand. She's never gotten emotionally involved with any guy.

Without thinking about it, I walk into the living room, where Dad is sitting in his armchair reading *Fishing World*. Then, for the first time in years, I climb onto his lap and bury my head in his chest.

He puts down his magazine and hugs me. "You all right, Dom?" After a pause he asks, "Is it that Wes boy? I mean, Wes?"

I feel myself choking up, and I nod.

"You really like this kid, don't you?"

I squeak, "Mmm-hmm."

"You know, hon . . . if he hasn't stepped up to the plate by now, maybe he's not going to."

"I just know he likes me, Daddy, even if he doesn't know."

"I'm sure he likes you. Mom and I both thought he liked you when we met him."

"Really?" I almost smile. "But then why . . . ?"

"Maybe he's intimidated. Guys can be real cowards."

"Intimidated?" I sit up and wipe my eyes with my knuckles. "Please. I am *so* nothing special."

"Nothing special?" Dad roars. Then he clears his throat and goes on more calmly. "Dominique, you do well in school, you're a beautiful girl, and, most important, you're a fabulous daughter and friend. That's pretty damned special in my book."

I shake my head no in response.

He asks, "In what way do you think you're not good enough for this kid?"

"It's just that . . . I'm starting to realize I don't even know if I *like* myself. I have no idea who I am, and there's nothing I enjoy doing all that much." I point to my Science Quiz certificates on the mantelpiece. "Take SQ. I just do it because it looks good on my résumé, and it's the only club at Shorr where I can contribute something. I don't genuinely care about it, though. I don't have any real hobbies."

"You have hobbies! You love biology! I thought you were pretty sure about becoming a doctor."

I take a deep breath and say, "Do I want to be a doctor? Do I really *want* to be a doctor? I know I've been saying I do all along. But now I'm starting to think it was just . . . inertia leading me down that path. If medicine really was for me, wouldn't I be tearing through medical journals in my spare time? Or volunteering at hospitals? I don't even watch *ER*! If being a doctor were my true calling, wouldn't I be thinking about it at least as much as I think about Wes?"

66

Dad smiles. "You know what? I think it's good you're confused about the future. That means you're open to more possibilities. I like being a policeman, but I wish I had taken more time to explore my options instead of jumping into the academy straight out of college. You don't need to have your life planned out right now."

"I'm not asking to have my life planned out, I just want a life! Wes is only a year older than me, but he's thinking about so many things other than me, like track and training for the New York City Marathon, and he reads at least one or two books a week. But he's all I seem to think about, all I want to think about. It's like I have no control anymore over what I *can* think about, and it's so exhausting. . . . But I *want* him, Daddy! And I want him to want me!"

I start bawling at full throttle. I must look like a two-year-old throwing a tantrum, but it also feels good to let it all out. A few minutes later, when my wails wind down to sniffles, Dad asks, "Hey, Dom, do you . . . do you really feel you, you know, *love* this guy?" He chokes on "love" as if there were a peanut shell stuck in his throat, but just hearing the word instantly causes me to stop crying, as if I'm having an epiphany.

Until now, for some reason, it has never occurred to me I might actually *love* Wes. I knew I really, really liked him and wanted to date him, but it seems illogical that I could *love* a boy I've spent only a few hours alone with, especially when I'm not sure about his feelings for me. On the other hand, I do want to be with him every minute, and I'm always going out of my way to do nice things for him, and the thought of his not wanting me makes me cry.

I guess I do love him. A lot.

I nod.

"Hmmm . . . Well, it's a pisser your first time's not a happy one, but you don't need a boyfriend right now, anyway. Just like you shouldn't commit to a career too early, you shouldn't commit to a guy so young."

I don't say anything and lean against him a few more minutes. Eventually I mumble, "I promised Mom I'd clean up the kitchen before she gets back. I'd better go do that."

"Go ahead, but keep your chin up. You never know what tomorrow will bring."

As I'm wiping off the countertops I start to feel rejuvenated. Dad's right. I *don't* know what tomorrow will bring, which is all the more reason not to rule out Wes. Even though I met him just a couple months ago, I feel more deeply for him than anyone else I've known for years. Truth be told, Wes is the first thing in my life I've ever felt totally, completely, and viscerally passionate about and want to devote every hour of my day to. I know that sounds off the wall, but I never knew I could be this into something, or someone. What's more, I've worked hard for everything I've ever earned in the past, be it good grades or SAT scores. I owe it to myself to work just as hard to win Wes's heart. Even Emily Dickinson wrote, "To love is so startling it leaves little time for anything else."

I rush to my room, turn on my computer, and allow the adrenaline to ooze from my fingertips as I compose my most personal e-mail yet, just short of declaring my eternal love. I write Wes that I'm so grateful for his friendship because he's the most interesting and talented guy I've ever met. I say a day isn't complete when I don't hear from him, and a week is empty if I don't see him at least once. I finish by telling him he's one of the closest friends I've ever had, but in my heart I'm wondering if he could be even more than that.

I opt not to proofread because I don't want to give myself the chance to edit down my emotions. I press SEND, inhale deeply, and resume writing my English paper with vigor. Of course, I still manage to check e-mail every three minutes for Wes's response.

12

It never comes.

Obviously, he doesn't want me as a girlfriend, and I had to push it. I think about writing him another e-mail telling him I'm okay with being just friends, but I know that would be a lie. I should be relieved, though. Now I have more time to ponder really important things, like current events. A huge segment of the world's population is dying of starvation, disease, natural disasters, and war. With all this tragedy happening around me, how can I justify being upset over somebody as trivial as a sprinter on EFM's track team? Anyway, it's not like Wes and I are breaking up. We've just stopped being friends.

On the second day of no reply, I ask Dad to time me as I play Operation in a feeble attempt to rekindle my interest in medicine and forget about Wes, even if just for a few seconds. But my hands are shaking so much I can't even tweeze out one piece without sounding the buzzer. I never realized before that this red-nosed patient is suffering from unrequited love too. He has a butterfly in his stomach, and his plastic heart is broken. My God, I'm actually identifying with the man in Operation. How much lower can I go?

On the third day, I don't have the patience to deal with my Shorr friends' cafeteria antics, so I have lunch by myself on one of the benches behind the school. Someone must have tipped off my mom, because soon she sits next to me and asks what's wrong. When I tell her, she says, "Oh, Dommie, three days is nothing to worry about!"

How can I make her understand the last three days may as well have been three centuries?

Then she urges me to recall my SAT prep course last summer and the cardinal rule for dealing with impossible multiple-choice questions.

"I know what you're getting at, Mom. *Cancel and move on.*"

"Exactly. I say that's what you should do with this young man. Now, I know it must be nice to have a crush on someone, but if he's not reciprocating, *cancel and move on.*"

I look at her and remember how she had no serious love interests before Dad, and Dad made his feelings for her clear from the beginning. Mom was never once in my position of aching for a boy she couldn't have, so she could never empathize with what I'm feeling. It's no wonder she teaches math. She thinks everything's so methodical and logical. To her Wes is no more significant than an irrational number or division by zero.

On the fourth day, Amy insists on taking me out to the mall as a "reality check." We're sitting in the food court when she says to me, "Look around, Dom. Hundreds of people. None of them knows who Gersh is. None of them cares. Look at that guy. And that guy. And that guy. They're all cute. They'd all probably think you're cute too."

This young couple sitting in front of Salad Shack catches my eye. They're sharing lemonade and exchanging kisses and smiles after every few sips.

"I want that," I say as I point to the canoodling pair, "but only with Wes."

Amy shakes her head. "My mom's worked with hundreds of dysfunctional couples who mistook raging hormones for love and are so obviously wrong for each other. You don't want to end up like that. Better to find out sooner than later."

"You encouraged me to pursue him, Ames. You said he was a great guy and that he was into me!"

"Yeah, but how did I know things would get this screwed up? I'm sorry to take your parents' side on this, but you have to get on with your life."

It's scary how my quasi breakup with Wes has made me feel more detached from Amy than ever before. I hate Wes for it. Just to spite him I order a Philly cheesesteak from the food court. After so many weeks of not eating meat, just the sight of all that fatty, cooked flesh makes me queasy, but I force myself to swallow every sinew anyway. That night I get diarrhea.

On the fifth day of no e-mail and with no recourse left, I actually call my grandma. I'm hoping confiding my troubles in her like I used to years ago will magically bring to life the feisty, problem-solving woman she used to be. Instead, all she says is, "He'd probably like you a lot more if you had better posture." Then she launches into stories of her own dating woes and complains how hard it is to find a man at her age. It's so demoralizing to hear a seventy-four-year-old woman who contributes nothing to society yearn for a boyfriend as if she were a teenager. What if I'm genetically destined to end up like her?

When night falls on the sixth day of not hearing from Wes, I wait until my parents' door is closed and they're sound asleep. After checking my e-mail for the trillionth time that week, I curl up in the fetal position and cry my eyes out. I catch a glimpse of myself in my full-length mirror, and I really do look like a baby, what with all the tears and snot dripping down my tomato red face and onto my sheets and pajamas. I almost laugh at the ridiculously pathetic image.

I don't know how I became such a wreck in a few short weeks. I wish I'd never laid eyes on him. I wish I could kill all the cells in my brain that store my memories of him so I could return to that happy, benign place where the foremost things on my mind were grades and Science Quiz. I was perfectly content being Amy's celibate sidekick. Now I may never be content again.

Finally I doze off with an empty hopelessness. When the phone wakes me up, I'm pissed to the core that my sleep—the only time of day when I'm not completely depressed—

has been interrupted. I grab my cell as if it were a weed and gaze disdainfully at the caller ID display. I don't for a second consider it could be Wes calling.

But it is.

He and I exchanged numbers back in January, but there was never any point in calling each other since our schedules were so conflicting. Also, we had been corresponding so well through e-mail, up until this week, at least.

My heart reels and I wait three more rings to make sure I'm not in a dream. I haven't the slightest idea what he's going to say. Maybe he wants me to return the *Runner's World* magazine he lent me. But would he phone me for that?

"Hello?" I try to sound calm even though I'm shaking.

"Hey," his voice radiates out from the earpiece. "Sorry for calling this late."

"It's okay," I say, faking a yawn as I check my clock. "Eleven's not that late for a Friday. Um, what's up?"

"I just made a disconcerting discovery. None of my e-mail went out all week."

"What?" I almost shout.

"I realized it today when my English teacher said she didn't receive my last paper. I upgraded my software Saturday, and since then all the e-mails I sent just got saved as drafts."

"Oh . . . That sucks!"

"I don't know how I screwed it up, but I messed around with a few settings and it's all fixed now." His voice starts to sound nervous. "So I wanted to call and tell you, in case you were wondering."

"Um, yeah. Thanks. I just assumed you were busy . . . or there really wasn't anything in my last e-mail to respond to."

"Of course I wanted to respond. I mean . . . there was a lot I wanted to say to you. Um . . . why weren't you at the meet on Tuesday?"

"Oh. I think that was the day I helped Amy proofread her lab report," I lie. "I'm sorry."

"It's okay, but my parents were missing you. So was I."

"Yeah? Well, I missed you all too," I manage to articulate, even though the corners of my mouth are the widest apart they've ever been. "Um, has everything you meant to send been sent to me?"

"Nah, I deleted everything, since so much time had passed. And I'd been wondering why you weren't writing back, and I got a little paranoid."

Me too! I want to shout. "Well, send me a summary tomorrow, okay?"

"Okay. One of the highlights was that I finally got a summer job. Southwest Florida College is hiring me as a library clerk."

"Congrats! That's funny, because I just found work too, as a receptionist at Amy's mom's practice. So . . . we'll both be in town this summer."

"Cool." Then a silence. "Anyway, I'm beat from practice, and I need to get to bed soon."

"Oh, okay. Well, thanks for calling."

"Sure. Sorry again about this, Dom. Bye."

There's no way I can sleep, and after ten minutes of giggling like a maniac, I find myself at the computer. I start crying again while I type.

Subject: I don't know . . .

Date: Saturday, March 2, 12:35 a.m.

Yes, I'm aware we just got off the phone, but I have to tell you something. This week was the first time in a while we weren't talking on a daily basis . . . and I felt sort of awful. I tried my best to block you out of my mind, but I couldn't. Then I kept wishing I'd never gone to that student-teachers football game in the first place. Hell, I don't know what I'm saying. If you only knew what I didn't write.

Do you want to come over tomorrow (which is really later today)? You haven't been to my place yet, so I think it's about time I play host and you play guest. I just bought a vegetarian cookbook, and it has a yummy-looking strawberry brownie recipe maybe we could make together. It'd certainly be a nice change from all those protein shakes and energy bars.

Your friend forever, Dominique

Subject: I don't know either . . .

Date: Saturday, March 2nd 1:02 a.m.

Dom,

I can't find the right words. I'm not sure exactly what I'm feeling, but I know I've never felt it before. I need to think about this a while longer before I can reply accurately and completely, but until then, just know I think about you a lot too. So if I look dazed when I come over tonight . . . 8-)—A grinning Wes

PART II

13

Saturday night. Wes rings my doorbell at 5:17. Thirteen minutes early. I'm wearing frayed cutoffs and my new see-through pink and green flower peasant blouse over a tank top. Wes looks adorable in khaki shorts and his EFM track and field T-shirt. My parents just left for the annual Fort Myers law enforcement banquet at the Sheraton and won't be back until after eleven.

I lead Wes to the kitchen and immediately put him to work on the brownies. I'm anxious about what might happen between us, so I'm glad we have an activity to ease us into the night and we're not forced to sit around and talk right away. While I measure out the ingredients, he mixes everything together in a big silver bowl. It's fun feeling this grown-up and domestic, almost as if we're some old married couple hanging out at home. I laugh when some flour gets on his face.

"You look like a coke addict with bad aim," I giggle.

In retaliation he throws a fistful of baking powder at me. Mid-getaway I slide on some spilled water and collide with the refrigerator door. That really cracks Wes up, and I join in the laughing fit. We must be releasing nervous tension or something because we can't stop laughing for at least three minutes.

After we pop the brownies in the oven and clean up the kitchen, I give Wes my "fifty-cent tour." We're done in a fraction of the time it took Wes to show me his house because one, my apartment is smaller, and two, I'm eager to get to my room. When we do, I already have a playlist of my favorite MP3s playing softly on my computer.

Wes stretches out on my carpet and says he's so glad this never-ending week is finally over.

"Amen," I respond as I sit on the floor facing him, my back resting against the foot of my bed.

So the stage is set, but I'm not sure what comes next. Neither of us has mentioned our latest round of e-mails, even though I know we're both thinking about them. I hate how it's so much easier to be open and straightforward to a computer screen than to an actual person.

Wes notices the poster hanging on the back of my door. "Who's that dude?"

"Oh. That's a portrait of Herophilus."

"Oh, him," he says sarcastically.

I laugh. "He was an anatomist back in 300 BC, but he was way ahead of his time. I wrote about him in my college essays on why I want to be a doctor."

Wes nods, but he looks sort of uncomfortable and is massaging his left shin. "I could use a doctor. I overdid it yesterday at practice."

I take my copy of *Gray's Anatomy* off the shelf. "Want to see which of your muscles is sore?"

"Yeah, sure." Then he laughs. "You read this stuff for fun, huh? I prefer Stephen King and Tom Wolfe."

"Yeah." I sit down by his right side. "I guess I never grew out of picture books."

I prop *Gray's* on my lap and angle it toward Wes. "This is a diagram of the leg, see?"

"Wow. My, um, gas-troc-nemius must be what's hurting," he says, pointing to the calf area. "Cool. I didn't know we had a muscle actually called the Achilles tendon. I thought it was just a nickname, like *funny bone*."

I flip the page to a full-body view of the muscular system.

He flinches. "I'm glad we have skin to cover all of that."

"Is this grossing you out? Sometimes I forget some people don't have the stomach for this type of thing. Amy never did."

"No, it's okay. It's cool seeing what's underneath."

"Yeah," I say, trying to catch his eye, "it is."

Wes lies flat on his back again. After reshelving the book, I sit next to him so we're both facing the same way, except I'm leaning back on my elbows—I know this position makes my 34Bs look bigger. I purposely didn't put my hair up in a ponytail tonight so it would spill all over my shoulders.

We remain silent as the sun continues to set. Amazingly, the mood's not that awkward tonight. It's kind of nice we can space out together without it feeling boring. Gradually the room darkens to black, and the only light comes from my computer's "starfield" screen saver. Soon the aroma of baking brownies envelops us, and the air-conditioning currents brush the ends of my hair lightly over his chin. Now Dave Matthews's "Crash" comes on. My mouth is literally watering, Wes smells so good right now.

I can tell something's about to happen, the same way you just know someone is looking at you or that you're going to get an electric shock if you touch the doorknob.

He raises his right hand and reaches over my left shoulder, but then he puts it back down.

"I'm sorry," he says.

"Why? What is it?"

"No, it's just—"

"Just what?"

"Just . . . your hair."

"My hair?" Is he annoyed by my hair touching his face?

"Yeah, I love the color. I can almost see it in the dark. I like it even better than Jessica's."

I'm not sure whether he's referring to his dog or his childhood friend, but I don't ask for clarification.

He continues, "Your hair was the first thing I noticed about you."

"Thanks, I inherited it from my mom," I tell him. "I like your hair too. It's so blond and sunny."

"Thanks . . . Dom?"

"Yeah?"

"I—Damn." He sits up cross-legged and shakes his head.

"What's wrong?"

Wes leaps to his feet and walks to my window. "This is embarrassing."

"What is?" I smile, knowing we're getting somewhere.

"I want to do something. I've been wanting to do something for a long time. It's just that . . ."

I don't prod him. I just wait.

After a few seconds he continues, "Dom, as you may have deduced, I've never . . . gone out with anyone before."

"Really?" My heart jumps. "No, I didn't deduce."

"Well, it's more than that. I've never . . . done it, or done anything. Heh, maybe that's my Achilles heel," Wes mutters, his voice drenched in vulnerability. Then he turns around and leans against my windowsill. "And the fact I've never done anything stops me from ever trying anything."

"Oh," I say, genuinely surprised, and pleased. "So, you've never done, like, *anything*?"

"I think you'd be surprised at how little play we dudes get. We make up such bullshit," he says defensively.

"Hey, I don't have much experience either," I say as I stand up.

"Much?" Wes is still facing the window but looks at me over his shoulder. I can barely see him in the darkness. Only his blue eyes reflect the computer light. "So, you've . . . kissed before?"

"Well, just a few superquick ones at camp and parties and stuff, but they don't really count since I didn't like the guys. Um, haven't there been any girls you wanted to kiss?"

Wes turns back toward me but looks at the floor. "Sure there were girls, but, I don't know, I was too chickenshit to try, or else they had boyfriends, or they were pretty but lacking any sort of personality, so I didn't think it was worth the effort . . . or we were friends and I was scared to screw that up."

"Yeah." I nod. "I understand."

"But, Dom . . ." He lifts his head and looks straight at me. "There's never been a girl I wanted to kiss as much as I want to kiss you right now."

Happiness. Joy. Ecstasy. Elation. Heaven. Nirvana. What-ever you want to call it, this is it. The totally, completely, and absolutely sublime euphoria of reciprocation. I swear it feels like I'm floating.

"Okay. Cool. I mean . . ." I force the words around my pounding heart. "I would like that. I want that too."

Wes marches toward me, grabs my shoulders with both hands, and kisses me. It's dry, soft, and still, but powerful.

When he releases me a couple seconds later, a jubilant, conquering look washes across his eyes.

"Wow." He smiles, his voice emboldened. "Dom, I'd like to do a lot more of that with you. Would that be okay?"

It takes all my self-control to stop myself from jumping up and down like a five-year-old. I can't believe the most perfect boy I've ever met in my life is saying this to me. *To me!* "Yes," I laugh, "that'd be okay."

"Dom?"

"Yeah?" I tremble.

Please say that I'm beautiful, that you love me, that it was love at first sight!

"Um . . . I think I smell something burning."

14

"Ames, you there?" I press my ear to the phone as I spin around in my swivel chair.

"Am I here? Am I here? I'm having convulsions on the floor, but yeah, I'm here. Oh, wow." I hear Amy setting down her brush and ripping off her smock. "Thank God, Dom. I was seriously starting to worry he was gay or asexual or something. Turns out he was just a rookie."

"I was worried he secretly liked that Jessica Sky girl . . . but he likes *me*!"

"Hold on a minute. This all happened last night? You waited a whole frickin' day to tell me?"

"I'm really really sorry about that. This morning, I don't know, I was just processing everything. Then I had to deal with going to Grandma's. My family doesn't even know yet."

"Okay, okay. So, the brownies are burning . . ."

"Well, after that it was pure chaos for two minutes. Our smoke detector went off, so Wes raced to open the terrace door, and I threw open the kitchen windows and turned on the oven fan. The brownies were like charcoal, and it took an hour for the smoke to clear. I was scared the sprinklers would go off, but Wes said it would have to get a lot hotter for that to happen."

"Did things get 'a lot hotter' between you two? A little *stove-top stuffing* in the kitchen?"

"Yeah, right. For a while we were just sitting on the couch in the living room, and he tried to make me feel better by telling me how when his family lived in Charleston, his brother, Arthur, accidentally burned down their garage with a dropped cigarette. Eventually I calmed down, and then . . . we *made out* until eleven!"

"Sweeeeet! How far did you get? Did he come in his pants?"

"No!" I laugh at her relentless vulgarity. "Nobody, you know, came. We did nothing below the neck."

"No Big O? Too bad."

"There was nothing 'bad' about it. I had no idea making out was so fun."

"Isn't it, though? Aren't boys' tongues so warm and wet and spongy?"

"Well, that sounds gross, but yeah, it was nice. I was

surprised how . . . natural it felt, how easy it was to get into the rhythm of it. I mean, we were just kissing normally for a few minutes and the next thing I know I'm pressing my tongue into his mouth."

"So Gersh is a good kisser?"

"Totally! I mean, I think he is. The first few seconds were weird, I guess because it was so new, and our teeth kept knocking together. But soon we were sucking face just like they do in the movies."

"When are you going at it again?"

"Well, he has track every day this week, so we can't see each other until Friday night, which sucks. But . . . he did send me a rather effusive e-mail today."

"Yeah? Let's hear it!"

"Okay," I chirp giddily as I punch it up on my computer. "The subject line is 'Hey, beautiful,' dated today, Sunday, March third. Um. 'Dear Dom, I'm sorry this will be short. E-mail is so empty, so sterile, so . . . well, it's nothing like the real thing, because there's nothing really there—no smells, no tastes, nothing to feel or listen to. Just weightless characters on a faceless screen.' "

"Oh my God, Dominique, what a poet! No wonder he's gonna major in English."

"There's more, hold on. 'I can't even count the number of times today I stopped in my tracks (pun intended) and shook my head, smiling as I replayed last night in my mind again and again. Dom, you are all at once the subject, object, predicate, preposition, and period of my thoughts (can you tell I've paid attention in grammar class?). Wes. P.S. My parents guessed about us. At breakfast this morning they said I looked so "pale and wan" that a pretty Shorr girl had to be the culprit.' Then he put a smiley face."

"I'm melting, I'm melting," Amy shrieks, mimicking the Wicked Witch of the West. "I can already see the headline of the EFM *Examiner:* 'Strong and Silent Sprinter Swaps Spit with Shorr Science Quiz Savant.' "

"Ha ha."

An hour later, after Amy and I hang up, I reread Wes's e-mail a few more times and look at myself in my full-length mirror. One of the best parts of hooking up with Wes is my battle-scarred appearance afterward. My lips are swollen from kissing him so much. My cheeks and chin are red and raw from rubbing against his stubble. When he left last night, my hair looked like it had been through a blender from his running his fingers through it, and it took forever to brush out. But I love it all—I am Wes-ed, Wes-inated, Wes-erized. I know that sounds strange, but I mean it. Suddenly my body is good for something more than just carting me around—it means something to someone else. I have never felt this alive and healthy before, and despite what Amy says, I can't imagine feeling more orgasmic than I do right now.

15

The next morning I slink into the dining room to break the news to my parents. I'm actually excited to hear their reaction because I know it's the last thing they expect. I take in a lungful of air and begin.

"Um, guys, I have to talk to you."

"Yes, sweetie?" Mom responds indifferently as she spreads cherry preserves over her toast. Dad doesn't seem to hear me at all as he skims the morning paper.

"Well, just so you know . . ."

Wes and I are going together. Uh-huh, we're a couple. The most handsome and brilliant guy in Florida wants me, and I want him too. In some ways, I think I love him more than I do you two. I certainly think about him more than I think about you guys.

"Saturday night, you know, two nights ago, remember you were at that banquet and I told you Wes came over and we made brownies? Well, we talked a lot, and we decided to, um, go out. So we're going out."

Mom and Dad exchange glances and then look up at me. I've actually stunned them into silence. Then Dad says, "Could he have spiked the brownies?"

"Very funny."

I flee to Shorr before they can make any other comments that might puncture my high. But that evening when I'm back home at my computer, Dad knocks on my bedroom door.

"Come in," I call as I turn off my monitor to hide my latest e-mail in progress to Wes.

He enters beaming. "I just wanted to say congratulations again on your victory today, hon!"

"You mean finally getting a date?"

Dad smiles. "I mean Science Quiz, my little champion."

"Thanks, Dad." Truth is, I am pretty pleased with myself for helping win our last tournament, though I'm not shedding any tears over the end of SQ. It can only mean more time to spend with my new favorite extracurricular.

"Hey, don't I get a hug?" he asks, extending his arms.

"Yeah, sure." I reluctantly turn away from my computer and go to him.

After kissing Wes that weekend, touching my father suddenly feels weird. I don't know why it should, it's just

Dad. But then again, he's a guy too, with a penis. Ick! I simulate hugging him by placing my limp hands on his shoulders and tensing up my arms. The second he releases me I retreat to my desk chair. Maybe I'm getting too old for our bear hugs.

Dad takes a seat on the foot of my bed. "So, Dom, now that Science Quiz is over, do you think you'll have time to go fishing in Sanibel with Mom and me this Saturday?"

"You know I don't fish anymore. Plus, I'll be seeing Wes."

"Yeah . . . about that Wes kid." Dad rests his elbows on his knees and puts his preachy face on. Obviously, this is what he came in here to talk about. "Dom . . . in some way, I'm actually damned proud of you because I know how much you wanted him, and you didn't stop till you got him. I was wondering why you were so happy yesterday, and I gotta tell you, it's great to see you like this. . . . Just promise me you'll be smart about . . . just don't let him pressure you into doing anything you shouldn't be doing. And you shouldn't be doing much, got it?"

"Sure, Dad." I give him a serious look and nod, praying he's not going to go into more detail.

"And you know you can talk to your mom and me about anything, right?"

"Yep." I nod more vigorously, hoping he'll get the hint and leave.

"By the way, why didn't he come to your match today?"

"Dad, he had track practice, and it's really bad to miss that. Anyway, he'd never expect me to miss SQ for a meet. . . . Was that question meant to make me doubt him?"

"Dom." He shakes his head. "I was just curious. I was looking forward to seeing him again now that you two are, um, dating."

"Okay." I turn back to my computer. "Dad, I need to finish some homework now. I'll come in for dinner soon."

Later that night Grandma calls to congratulate me on the SQ finals, the broadcast of which she watched on a local TV station. Last time we spoke on the phone she made me feel like a hunchbacked alien for being single, so I assume the recent progress in my love life will please her.

"Is he going to be a doctor or lawyer?" she asks as soon as I mention Wes.

I roll my eyes. "I think most doctors and lawyers are kind of old for me, Grandma."

"I just want someone who can provide for you, sweetheart."

"Well, maybe *I'm* going to be the doctor in the family."

"If you're a doctor, then how will you have the time to make a home for your husband and take care of children?"

"Anyway," I huff, counting to five to refuel my patience, "this boy's so nice and incredibly smart. He's a track star."

"A what star?"

"You know, running? Like in races."

"Does he try to have intercourse with you?"

"Grandma!" I gasp. "Not that it's any of your business, but no!"

"Good. Remember, no ring, no ring-a-ding-ding. Because once you spread your legs for him, do you know where he'll race once he's done? He'll race to another woman, that's where. I expect my only granddaughter to wear white to her wedding and for it not to be a sham. If he loves you, he'll wait."

"Y-you know what?" I stammer, my face suddenly hot. "I thought you'd be happy for me. Instead, you're telling me to dump him for a lawyer, that I shouldn't work, and that he's going to leave me if we have sex? Please! I'm going now, and hopefully I'll forget how you ruined my good news like you always ruin everything. Goodbye!" I flip down the cell.

A few seconds later Mom bounds into my room. "Are you okay, Dommie? We heard yelling."

"Yeah, I'm fine. It's just that, God, Mom, I was in such a good mood too. Grandma drives me crazy sometimes."

"You're lucky you have one, though. Remember that."

After Mom leaves I lie down and punch a pillow. Maybe I was unduly horrible to her and should apologize. She really didn't say anything all that bad. She's just old-fashioned. And lonely. Before I met Wes, I guess I was lonely too. I mean, I suppose I was happy enough, but now that I think about it, I don't remember about what.

I swallow my pride and dial her number.

16

Going to school Friday is pointless. I feel like a wild animal at a zoo, except the cages are made of windowless walls, lockers, bulletin boards, and splintery brown doors leading to dead-end classrooms, where poor schoolteachers who have given up on their own lives and probably haven't gotten laid in years find their only pleasure in testing us on depressing subjects. I resent having to learn about *Crime and Punishment,* the slave trade, and the division of cancer cells when all I want to think about is Wes.

I know there's no way I can finish out the day without going crazy, so I skip my last period, P.E., and pedal home as fast as I can, fueled by my growing excitement about commencing the second weekend of Wes and me as a couple. I luxuriate in the world's longest, most thorough shower and spend forever on the phone with Amy, trying to decide which bra and panties set I should wear. We settle on my white cotton with lace trim.

My hair is done, my makeup's applied, and my pink sundress is on by six o'clock, an hour early. I count away the final minutes while I sit in front of my air-conditioning vent because I'm sweating in anticipation of seeing my boyfriend. *My boyfriend!*

I say a quick good night to my parents, assuring them I'll be back by one, and I dash downstairs without giving them the opportunity to say more than "Goodbye, be careful!"

"I will," I call back.

Wes is right on time. Just seeing his blue Explorer turn the corner onto my street makes my stomach flip.

When I climb into his passenger seat and proclaim, "Why, hello there!" he responds with a quick "hey" and a blank expression. Then silence. I'm suddenly completely disoriented. We tongue-kissed for three hours straight last Saturday, and he wrote me five beautifully cheesy e-mails since then. So why does he look like someone died? Was the other night a fluke?

After three blocks of deafening quiet, Wes mutters, "So, where do you want to go?"

"Oh. Um, I'm not sure." I force a weak grin, trying to salvage some of the good feeling I had all day. But now that he mentions it, I'm not sure what tonight is supposed to be. Does he want to go grab a bite to eat somewhere? Or does he just want to make out again? Or neither?

"Um," I continue, "I mean, we can do whatever. We can

get takeout and watch something at my place, but my parents are home, so we can't . . . well—"

"My parents are home too, and I'm not hungry."

"Well, I don't know, then."

"I think I know of someplace."

I want to ask him where, but he looks weirded out, almost upset, so I don't want to pester him with questions. Instead, I sit back in the seat and stare out my window, watching the ugly strip malls race by and bracing myself for the worst.

Fort Myers hugs the Gulf Coast, so there are a ton of docks. Some of them are really fancy with big yachts lined up in neat rows, and others are old industrial sites that can get pretty sketchy. Wes pulls into the parking lot of a dock that's definitely one of the latter, and we're the only ones here besides a few scraggly seagulls. Maybe Wes does want to make out. Or maybe he wants to tell me it's over, and he chose a secluded spot in case I make a scene.

After he parks, I break our four-mile silence. "Not to be a drag, but you're sure this place is safe?"

"It's not like we're in the South Bronx, Dom."

"I know, I know. But still." Dad's always reminding me how Fort Myers has a significant crime rate for a midsized city, so I'm a lot more conscious of these things than the average suburban teen.

Wes says, "Paul told me he sets off sparklers here sometimes and that no one ever comes by."

"Okay. I guess it's fine, then."

More silence. Just the hum of the engine. He's not touching me. He's not even looking at me. That's it. He's not into me anymore. I want to die.

"Dom?" he says, staring straight ahead.

"Yes?" I choke.

"I actually barfed this morning I missed you so badly."

"What?" I burst out laughing, utterly relieved.

Wes looks down at his lap and shakes his head. "This week was torture. All I wanted was to be alone with you again, to make sure it was real. I can't believe I'm somebody's boyfriend."

"Yeah, I know what you mean." I make a mental note that when Wes looks sad, it's not necessarily because he's upset with me. He's distant and withdrawn because he misses me, not because he doesn't. Then I muse, "It's strange, Wes, I . . . I feel like we should be going out to dinner and a movie, a traditional date or something. And that we should be, you know, talking. Talking about us and stuff and making plans. But we've been talking for weeks, and now that we're alone . . ."

Wes turns to me and looks into my eyes. "I don't want to *talk,* Dom."

With that, he turns off the engine, and my body switches to autopilot.

17

I lean over and kiss Wes on the mouth. Then I crawl onto his lap. Soon we're Frenching and holding each other just like we did on my couch last week. I love how comfy and familiar everything suddenly feels between us, but I think we're both a little nervous too, especially Wes. His palms are really sweaty, so he keeps having to wipe them across the cloth upholstery.

After beeping the horn by mistake, which for some reason elicits gut-splitting laughter from both of us, we migrate to the backseat and continue kissing. The windows are darkly tinted, so I feel invisible to the outside world, as if we're in our own private little cave. It's impossible to get comfortable, though. Wes is so tall he can barely move without knocking his head and feet against the door handles and window controls, and the seat belt catches keep digging into our thighs and torsos. Wes mentions the backseats can be moved, so we shift them forward and spread out in the expanded trunk space. This is the first time we're actually lying down together, and it definitely makes everything seem a lot more sexual.

I guess Wes feels it too because soon he's nibbling at my ears, which is actually really nice, like an unannoying kind of tickling. I had no idea that area of the body was so sensitive. Then without warning Wes bites my neck.

"Ouch, ooh!" I whinny.

"Oh, sorry." He pulls back. "Crap, I don't know what came over me. I'm so sorry, Dom!"

"No, it's okay. I liked it, really, just a little bit softer, maybe," I try to reassure him, not wanting him to clam up again. "Um, you can do it again if you want."

"Not if it hurts you."

"Well, if you don't, I will!"

I summon up all my impulsiveness, lean over, and gently gnaw at the depressed area over his left collarbone. It tastes . . . like nothing in particular. Maybe slightly salty.

"Mmmm," he says, "that is kinda nice. Good pain."

"Yikes!" I lean back. "Are we entering into the realm of S and M already?"

"I'll just call you Dominatrix," Wes says before lightly biting me again on my neck, then high on my chest. Soon I feel his hands start to explore my back. When his fingers reach the zipper of my dress, a part of me wants to say we should stop. A very small part. One that is easily ignored.

"Wes?"

"Yeah?" he practically pants.

"Do you want to . . . ?"

Wes freezes up and spurts, "Do I want to what?"

I sit up next to him. "It's okay if you want to take off my dress."

I hear him swallow nervously. "Yeah?" he breathes. "Do you want me to?"

I don't know where my audacity comes from, maybe from having fantasized about this moment for so many weeks, but I get up on my knees and unzip my sundress so the top part is hanging over my waist like an apron. I can almost feel his blue eyes piercing into my chest.

I slide my left forefinger under my left bra strap and ask, "So, I guess you've never tried taking one of these off a girl before, huh?

"Of course not." He smiles. "But I can try."

I lean toward him and we kiss again. Both his hands are on my back now as he reaches for my bra clasp. I can immediately tell he has no clue. He starts to tug on it a little, then move it up and down.

"Ouch," I squeal as his nails dig into my skin by mistake.

"Sorry. I'm such a loser. It's like trying to get out of Chinese finger cuffs."

"You just haven't had the practice. I've been taking these things on and off since I was eleven."

"Can you show me how? I mean, if that's all right."

"Um, yeah, that'd be fine."

I reach my hands behind my back. "You just grab the

two parts and pull them together a little." I unhook my bra but keep it on. "Voilà."

"How did you do that? Hook it and let me try again."

He reaches his arms behind me and starts fumbling some more, but soon he's exclaiming, "Hey, I got it! I got it!"

My back is bare, but my bra's still hanging on my shoulders concealing my breasts. Light from the distant dock lanterns penetrates the windows, casting a delicate blue sheen over us. We grin at each other softly, as if on cue. I get another sudden rush, like I know this is a moment I'll remember forever.

"Go ahead," I whisper, stunned this is actually happening.

Wes gets up on his knees and grabs both shoulder straps before indelicately yanking off the bra. I wish he had been a little more gradual, to make the moment last.

"Wow, Dom!" His eyes widen like saucers.

I think I was expecting to be embarrassed, but I'm not in the slightest. I *want* him to see me naked, physically and emotionally. In a fit of passion I reach over and hug him tightly, but instead of hugging me back he wedges his hands between our chests and starts feeling my breasts. Softly at first, then a little rougher, like he's trying to figure out what they can withstand. It's fantastic, invigorating, freeing. The sensation of his big, manly hands on my skin makes my whole body feel like silk. I'm so glad I never let anyone else touch me there before. It's as if I've been holding out for Wes before I even knew he existed. Still, I think again how this would be a good time to stop for the night, but then he asks if I want his shirt off too.

"Yeah, definitely!" I hear myself answer.

I grab the sides of his polo and start to tug. My breasts are still on full display, and I think he's a little mesmerized because he's not moving at all, just gazing. Undressing him reminds me of trying to change a sleepy, uncooperative four-year-old into his pajamas.

"Hey, can you just lift your arms up a little?"

"Oh, sorry, Dom."

I pull off his shirt, and he looks so good. Of course I've seen tons of guys topless at the beach and in magazines and stuff, but I've never gotten close enough to actually touch anything. I hesitate, not sure what to do, but then I slowly place my hands on his flat, almost concave stomach. It's hard and slightly hairy. I can feel it contract as he breathes. I don't think I'll ever enjoy reading *Gray's Anatomy* or playing Operation again, now that I get to handle a live specimen.

I glance at his face, and he's just watching me as I explore his torso. Things suddenly feel too serious and I want to lighten the mood, so I poke him in the tummy and say, "Nice six-pack, Gersh."

"Nice rack, Baylor."

"Wes!"

I start tickling him under his arms, and he laughs and squirms for a few seconds before rolling on top of me. I love the secure sensation of Wes's weight pressing down on my body, although it makes taking deep breaths a little difficult. Sometimes he gyrates his pelvis against mine, which would probably feel better if there weren't a layer of denim between us. Soon the temperature inside the car gets really hot and the windows fog up, so we have to stop for a moment while Wes turns on the engine and the air-conditioning. Then it begins pouring outside, which makes fooling around in the trunk of our cozy vehicular sanctuary all the more exhilarating.

After three hours of nonstop kissing and feeling up, I tell Wes I need a breather, so we lie in each other's arms in contented silence. I know this is only our second night together, but I can't stop thinking about sex, what it would feel like. It'd be nice to have some sort of climax to all this physicality, if only to feel like we're finished, like we'd done something whole and complete. But that would be a huge step from where we are now. Sex still feels like a fantasy, something that couldn't actually happen.

"So, what are you thinking about?" I ask him.

"I'm thinking that I love your voice."

Just say you love me! I'm bursting to say it, but I want you to do it first!

"My voice?" I ask.

He nods. "Now that SQ's over and you can stay up later, maybe we can talk on the phone at night. It'd be nice to hear you, not my keyboard."

"Wow, the telephone—what an archaic concept," I say sardonically. Then I smile at him. "You know what I'm thinking?"

"What?"

"That I love . . . your anatomy. It's perfect."

"Nah." Wes grins.

"Yes!" I sit up and look at him. "In class, we're always learning about the body in terms of, you know, breathing, eating, sleeping—"

"Sweating, barfing, farting," Wes interrupts, laughing.

I laugh too, though this is the second time tonight I'm reminded of bratsitting.

"Yes, all that too. But seriously, if you think about it, the body was made to show affection. Look." I point to his head. "Hair for me to run my fingers through."

Next I point to his baby blues. "To make eyes at me."

I continue to work my way down Wes's body.

"Your lips, to kiss me with. Your teeth, to bite me with. Your neck, for me to bite. Your arms, to hold me; your fingers, to caress me . . ."

I skip over his crotch and go right down to his feet. "To push the gas pedal with when you come by to pick me up. See, you're perfect!"

Wes grins even wider and says, "Dom . . . I still can't believe this is happening."

I can feel my stomach turn in on itself. I swear, I've gotten more highs this week than during my entire life up until Wes. "Well, let me try to convince you of the reality of the situation."

I snuggle under him and we resume kissing. I can feel his penis pressing through his jeans up against my inner thighs. If we were naked, we'd have been close to having sex missionary style. Almost without thinking about it I drag my right hand down his chest and abdomen until my fingers are over his jeans just below his belly button. Then I start walking my fingers down even farther. He's holding his breath and his heart is racing, sending vibrations into my own chest. I feel dizzy and light-headed, like every cell in my body is pushing my arm that final inch. I'm just about to rest my hand on his crotch when a thunderous bang echoes through the car.

Did he just ejaculate?

I pull my hand away from Wes's stomach as he leaps up, bumping his head on the fuzzy gray ceiling.

"What the hell was that?" he asks, looking to either side of him.

"Um, wasn't that you?" I figured he convulsed and kicked the trunk door when I touched him. I barely grazed his jeans, but Amy warned me that guys our age can come really easily.

"No," he whispers sharply. "It was from outside."

I slowly lift my head and see the dark outline of a man against the back windshield, his fist pressed into the glass.

"Oh shit, oh shit! Someone's there!" I shriek, my heart shooting out of my chest.

"Relax, stay calm!" Wes says firmly as he reaches for his polo, which I had rolled up to use as a pillow.

I can see the headlines: CARJACKER KILLS HALF-NAKED TEENAGERS.

Wes pulls on his shirt and presses his face to the glass.

"It's a cop. Fuck! I knew we shouldn't have left the car running."

I revise the headline: POLICE CHIEF'S DAUGHTER ARRESTED FOR LEWD AND OBSCENE BEHAVIOR. STANFORD TOSSES HER APPLICATION.

"Wait here," he says. "He's motioning for me to come out."

"Shit. Be careful," I whisper shakily.

I throw on my bra and sundress as Wes crawls over me and exits through the driver's side door. I peer through the side window and watch as the lone policeman talks to Wes and frisks him. Then the cop motions toward me.

As they walk toward the rear I smooth back my hair and slip on my sandals. The trunk door opens to me sitting cross-legged with a petrified look on my face. The cop peers inside. I raise my hand in a silly wave. I don't recognize him from the times I've visited headquarters. I hope he doesn't recognize me and that he doesn't ask for my ID or last name.

"Are you all right, miss?"

"Yes sir," I squeak, trying to disguise my voice.

"Come out," Wes instructs me, his pulse obviously going a mile a minute. "He asked if he could search the car for alcohol and stuff, and I said that'd be fine."

I quickly hop out of the trunk and take my place next to Wes, who's looking sheepishly at the ground. I look down also and hold my jacket over my head in an attempt to shield my eyes from the rain, which has downgraded to a cold drizzle. I'm so scared Wes's brother hid a stash of pot or something in the car back when he owned it and forgot about it. I want to cling to Wes's arm, but I'm too afraid to move.

After what seems like forever, the cop approaches us and stares us down. "It's pretty stupid of you to go parking here. What if some rapist or murderer got to you before I did? If you were my kids, I'd ground you for a year. Use your brains next time, got it?"

"Yes, officer," Wes and I recite in unison as we dart back into the car and tear out of the dock. My thoughts immediately turn to my parents. Dad would blow his top if he knew. Mom would be so embarrassed if this ever got out to the other teachers at Shorr. I know what my grandma would say: *How can you have a white wedding now?*

"I—I can't believe that just happened to us," I stammer, shivering in my damp clothes.

"He was right, though. I'm sorry, Dom. I should have known better."

"It wasn't your fault. I'd better get home, though. It's almost one."

I open the visor mirror to check my makeup, and I literally gasp at what's staring back at me. My neck is sprinkled with reddish purple contusions! I break into a giggling fit when I realize I was Wes-inated again. My first hickeys!

"What's so funny?" Wes asks.

"Look." I hold my hair up with my hands. "Don't worry, they don't hurt."

His jaw drops when he sees them. Then he smiles smugly. "Hey, do I have any?" he asks, tilting his head up.

"Yes!" I shriek. "You have a couple little ones, under your ear. I bet Paul and the other guys on the team will be teasing you like crazy at practice Monday."

"Great," he says sarcastically.

Then we both break out laughing. At the next red light, I lean over and hug him. "Between the smoke detector and this, we've had an exciting week."

"A little too exciting for my taste, but yeah, in retrospect it's pretty funny."

"Hey, even if some psycho killer did try to get us, you're so fit, you could've kicked his ass."

"Dom, it's really difficult to kick ass with a hard-on."

I giggle nervously, and I wonder how long it's going to be before I get a look at his hard-on. I'm also a little shocked he even said the word, but if tonight was any indication, he's growing out of his shyness fast. We both are.

When Wes drops me off at my building, we make out for a good five minutes in the front seat before I reluctantly go upstairs. I don't care that everyone driving by, including the cops, can see everything that's going on.

18

Now that parking in Wes's car is officially a bad idea, we're forced to consider alternative venues. Amy's lucky her mom and stepdad have season tickets or memberships to every sports team, museum, and dramatic arts center within a fifty-mile radius. They're always out on the town for hours at a time, and Amy can bring home her hookup du jour without anyone being the wiser.

Unfortunately, both Wes's and my parents swear by the "early to bed, early to rise" motto and stay home most evenings. But three days after we're busted by the cop, I propose a solution to Wes during one of our now nightly phone calls.

"So, do you remember when we were looking at your photographs, and you mentioned your grandparents in SoHo keep a condo on Captiva Island? What's it like?"

"Um, I dunno, it's nice for a studio. It's on the second floor, Gulf view. There's an indoor garage, no elevator. Why do you—? Oh." He chuckles. "I like how you think, Dom."

"If it's empty most of the time anyway, maybe you could figure out a way for us to get in?"

"Not sure, but I'll see what I can do."

"Good. I can't wait till this weekend, either way."

"Ditto."

On Friday evening at Wes's meet, I see his parents for the first time since we started going out. For all they know, Wes and I are already having sex, so I'm worried they'll see me as some sort of slut-ho corrupting their precious son. I beg Amy to accompany me as moral support, and I make sure to conceal my not-quite-faded hickeys with a strategically tied bandanna.

When we get to our seats, the Gershwins seem to be their typical happy, vaguely spaced-out selves, outfitted in their usual pastel sweatsuits.

"Hello, Dominique!" Mrs. Gershwin stands up and hugs me.

I hug her back, feeling a lot more secure about everything. I figure she wouldn't want to hug a slut-ho.

Then I shake hands with Mr. Gershwin, who says smilingly, "Good to see you, Dominique."

Amy says brightly, "Hey, Mrs. G, Mr. G. Long time, no see."

"Hello, Amy!" Mrs. Gershwin hugs her too. "So glad

you could make it. And what fine taste in best friends you have!"

Amy nods in agreement, and I blush.

"The team's been missing you, Braff," Mr. Gershwin says. "You were the best distance runner by a long shot."

"Thanks, Mr. G. I'm taking it up again at Amherst."

When we sit down, Mrs. Gershwin leans over to whisper in my ear. "We're so happy about you and Wesley. We knew from the first time we met that you were very special."

Chills race down my spine I'm so delighted. "Thank you, Mrs. Gershwin," I whisper back. "That's really nice of you to say."

Amy elbows me in a congratulatory way, and at the same moment Wes looks at me from across the field and winks. It's all so perfect I almost cry. Here I am with my amazing best friend, watching my amazing boyfriend, sitting next to his amazing parents, who obviously think I'm amazing. January and February were such an emotional purgatory, but it was so worth it, just for this moment.

The streak continues that night when Wes picks me up with a kiss and a key.

"You did it!" I cheer. "You didn't mention it, so I didn't know."

"I found it in Dad's desk and got it copied during lunch."

"You're so sneaky! And I'm so glad, because—" I open the flap of my knapsack so he can see the contents. "I bought a sheet from Target to cover the bed with so we won't have to worry about washing your grandparents' sheets."

He turns to me and grins. "Good thinking."

A half hour later we're in the studio. Wes keeps the lights on only for a moment so the power bill won't reflect any more electricity usage than necessary. In those few seconds I can see there's a small balcony that looks right onto the beach. The room is furnished with white wicker dressers and nightstands, a cedar and brass grandfather clock, peach-colored carpet and drapes, a mini dining room table, and, best of all, a huge white canopy bed. This will be the first bed we've ever been in together.

I unfold the new sheet and drape it over the comforter. Wes turns out the lights. Then I hear him lock the door.

Wes comes up behind me and cups my breasts in his hands. Almost as a reflex I reach behind me and rub the bulge in his shorts. Was our first kiss really just two weeks ago? Amy's told me how difficult it is to stop making out once things really get going. I never understood that before Wes, but it *is* really difficult to stop, or even just to take things slowly. Now that we've gone this far, I can't imagine there being a time when just a good-night kiss will be enough for either of us. And I hope it never is.

Wes and I kiss passionately, almost desperately, as we undress each other. He removes everything but my under-wear. I take off his T-shirt and sneakers. Soon we're on the bed with me on top. Then I sit up, straddling his thighs. He lies perfectly still as I unbutton and unzip his shorts. I'm assuming he has underwear on, so I don't hesitate as I quickly draw his shorts down below his hips.

"Whoa," I gasp like some shocked virgin, which I guess I am. I wasn't anticipating seeing his erect penis right away;

it's protruding up through the flap in his boxers and resting against his lower belly.

"What's wrong, Dom?" He looks down. "Shit, I'm sorry. I didn't know—" He reaches down to his boxers, but I gently stop his hand.

"No, it's okay." I try to give him a reassuring smile, but my heart is beating so fast I think my face is twitching.

Even by the dim blue moonlight filtering in through the glass balcony doors, I can recognize the features of his penis from my anatomy books. The shaft, the head, the urethral opening—it's definitely all there. Only it looks so much more alive and urgent than any photograph could ever capture. I lean forward over Wes's torso so I can study it head-on. Then I notice it bobbing up and down slightly with his heartbeat, as if it's waving me on. I sit back on his thighs and take a deep breath.

I don't feel ready to touch it just yet, so I start by easing my hands underneath his boxers and lightly rub the area surrounding it. His pubic hair is so long and coarse! It never occurred to me before that guys probably rarely trim this stuff, if ever. In Florida it's always bikini season, so I'm constantly shaving down there.

Wes murmurs something unintelligible and closes his eyes. He's obviously into this. Soon I close my hands in on his balls, but I'm not sure what to do with them. I've seen enough slapstick about guys getting kicked in the nuts to know they're ultrasensitive, so I pet them in a tickly, feathery way. This is by far the most delicate part of Wes I've come across yet—the consistency makes me think of a baby bird, or squishy nectarine skin, scattered with hair. It's

113

truly surreal to think I'm holding Wes's scrotum, his personal sperm generator.

Now I'm on the bed to the side of his left hip, and I ease his shorts and boxers down to his knees. As I sit there beholding the entire package, I picture myself in a Science Quiz match.

Now for the final question: Does a respectable and responsible seventeen-year-old girl stimulate the penis of her significant other in his grandparents' vacation home while their trusting parents think they are out bowling? . . . Ms. Baylor?

Hell yes!

I lightly clutch Wes's penis with my right hand and start to stroke it lightly, up and down the length of it. Back in middle school, Amy and I would always sneak into her mom's office and pore over her sex encyclopedia. I wish I had a better recollection of what it said about manual stimulation.

"Listen," I say softly, "I'm just sort of exploring. I have absolutely no idea what to do."

"That's fine, this feels great," he says hurriedly, over his heavy breathing.

I continue to stroke him, and it's cool how the skin can move up and down a little, like it's not really attached to whatever's underneath. I try to vary the speed and position of my hand, but Wes just continues to groan in the same, quiet way. After a few minutes of this exercise, I'm wondering why he hasn't ejaculated. Do you have to do something special to finish a hand job? I don't remember anything about grand finale techniques in the sex encyclopedia.

I guess Wes can tell I'm getting discouraged because he wraps his hands around mine and guides me through a few strokes. He says it responds well to pressure. When he releases his hold I tighten my grip.

"Hey, don't pull it off."

"Oh, sorry, sorry."

"And can you take off your ring? It chafes."

"Oh yeah, I should have thought of that." I reach for my purse and drop in the mood ring.

"You know what feels good? When you touch the tip."

"Oh, okay." I take him back in my hands.

"And, um, don't forget about these," he says while pointing to his balls.

I have to hold back laughter—I thought guys were supposed to be easy to get off.

Now my right hand is stroking his penis, and the other is caressing his testicles. I'm feeling very ambidextrous. I wonder if I'd ever be able to get my mouth around his penis if I tried. But that's definitely not going to happen tonight. Blow jobs are really serious business, and I'm not even sure what I'd need to do once I got down there. It's tricky enough with two hands.

After five more minutes, still nothing. My hands are now sticky from my own sweat, so my palms keep tripping up and getting stuck unevenly on his penis.

"Ugh, I'm terrible at this."

"No, no. You're doing great. I'm not lying."

"I feel like I'm hurting you. There's so much friction."

"Hey, could you lick your hands? Like, really salivate on them?" Wes has a desperate look in his eyes.

Even though the idea *completely* grosses me out, I give my palm a lick. I can already tell it's not going to be enough, so I generate some more saliva in my mouth and do it again. I can't bring myself even to look at my slobbery hand as I move it back to his dick, but it seems to do the trick.

"Okay, yeah, better, much better. Yeah," he moans. "Can you go faster?"

I can barely feel my arms now, and my shoulders are sore, but I take deep breaths and keep going. Every few seconds I alternate hands and lick them. "Hand job" is such a misnomer for this full-body routine. It's like I'm a one-man band.

Soon a few drops of something hot leak onto my fingers. Wes's breathing is getting heavier too, and suddenly he mutters breathlessly, "Tighter. Ah, Aah, Dom. Dom—"

I feel a stiffening of his penis in my hands as the tip expels a thick, creamy liquid. Wes's legs tremble and his back arches as he groans loudly. I discover the warm, white goo cascading down my knuckles serves as a great lubricant, so I stroke even faster.

"Dom . . . you can stop. . . . Stop now!" he almost shouts.

Taken aback by his tone of voice, I instantly let go of his penis, which begins to lose its stiffness and bend over to one side. After a few seconds Wes places his hand on my shoulder reassuringly.

"Sorry, Dom. It hurts if you keep doing it after I come."

"Oh, okay. I understand."

Wes takes one of the tissues from the nightstand and wipes the semen off his dick and stomach. I look down at my palms, now a deathbed for hundreds of millions of tiny sperm that never had the chance to pursue their singular purpose. But I don't feel guilty. In fact, I can't remember the last time I've felt such a sense of accomplishment.

After washing up in the bathroom, I crawl back into bed. Wes shudders when my cold hands touch his warm, sweaty abdomen.

"So, was that okay?" I ask, though I'm pretty sure it was.

"Um, let's see. *Yeah!*"

I look down and am startled how much smaller his penis is. It's a quarter of the size it was three minutes ago. He doesn't look embarrassed to be lying before me naked, though, which is cool. I'm glad I make him comfortable.

I say, "In movies, this is always when the guy rolls over and goes to sleep."

"Nah, I want to take my revenge first." Wes reaches his hand for my underwear, and I'm instantly scared. What if he can't make me orgasm? Or what if he can? In movies women make strange noises and even stranger facial expressions while it's happening. I don't think I want Wes to see me like that. What if I squeal or scream or fart or say something stupid?

"Hey, listen, you don't have to do it to me if you don't want to. I mean, I don't . . . I didn't do that expecting anything in return."

He screws up his eyebrows. "Are you kidding? I want to."

"Well, the thing is, I'm sorta having that bad time of the month." My period actually ended two days ago.

"Oh." He looks disappointed.

"I want to, but I'd rather wait till it's over."

"Yeah, that's okay. No worries, Dom."

Now I'm afraid I ruined the good mood, so I try to turn the conversation back to him. "I'm curious about something, though. When you were actually, you know, what did it feel like for you, when it was happening?"

"You mean when I came?"

"Yeah. Then."

"I dunno, it's hard to describe."

"I know, but I'm really curious what it's like for a guy to have one."

"Well, at first it feels sort of light and zingy, and then, *bam!*" He claps his hands together. "It's Chernobyl."

"Chernobyl?"

"Yeah, Chernobyl."

"Huh. So your orgasms are basically the physiological equivalent of a nuclear explosion at a Russian power plant?"

He laughs. "Yes, Ms. Science Quiz, it's a meltdown."

Wes climbs on top of me and rests his head on the flat space between my breasts. I keep one arm around his shoulders and massage his scalp with my other hand. I love this position. I feel protective and protected at the same time.

We lie like this until the grandfather clock strikes midnight. After we get dressed, we cover our tracks by smoothing out the bed and flushing the used tissues down the toilet.

19

I don't know if I simply forgot Wes told me he was going away for spring break, or if I blocked it out, not wanting to believe that we're going to be separated for nine whole days. Either way, ever since Wes reminded me his family will be vacationing with the Skys in Paris, I haven't been able to stop thinking about Wes and former girl next door Jessica running together along the banks of the Seine.

Amy says I have paranoia and insecurity issues and that if Wes misbehaves in Paris, then he's obviously wrong for me and I should be glad to find that out now before things go too far. That doesn't make me feel any better, though.

The Friday before the Gershwins leave for France, the air-conditioning at their home breaks. His parents decide to escape the heat by going to dinner and a community theater production of *Guys and Dolls* out in Naples. They ask us to come, but of course we decline so I can help Wes study biology. Yeah, right. We're jumping at the chance to mess around at his place and not have to trek out to Captiva.

As soon as the Gershwins drive away, Wes and I race upstairs, slide into his bedroom, and almost violently strip each other down to our underwear. I'm taking a second to lay my watch and mood ring on his nightstand when I catch sight of the other Jessica lounging on Wes's desk chair. She seems to be watching us intently, and we make eye contact. When Wes turns his back to switch off the lights, I stick out my tongue at her. *He's mine now, bitch!*

We're on the bed and I reach for his boxers, but he pushes my hands away. "No, you come first, Dom." Then we both laugh and he says, "I mean, you first tonight."

I nod and lie down on his bed. This time I feel ready.

Wes says, "I've only a vague concept of what I'm supposed to do. So I'll need some instruction."

"Actually, I'm just as clueless as you are."

He crinkles his brow. "Haven't you ever tried?"

"Huh?"

"You know what I mean."

"Um, not really." I blush. I'm embarrassed to admit I've been touching myself every day in the shower this past week, trying to psych myself up for this. It got to the point where it felt good, but never *Oh God-ly*. I can't figure out what I'm doing wrong. Maybe I'm just thinking about it too much, or I haven't been turned on enough when I'm by myself.

"Really? Never?" Wes asks.

"Yeah. . . . Do you, um—?"

"Yeah, of course. We dudes got to make sure everything's fully operational from time to time."

He lies down next to me and immediately reaches his right hand down under my panties. I'm ecstatic Wes is finally touching me there, but I also feel put on the spot. I'm not excited enough yet to enjoy this.

"Um, actually, this is a little fast. Could we, like, hug and kiss a little more first, before you—?"

His mouth comes down hard on mine, and he runs his hands all over my body. Soon he starts kissing my breasts, and I envision my fantasy of Wes chasing me on the beach and struggling to rip down my bathing suit.

And then he farts. Really loud.

He lifts his head and looks down at me awkwardly. "Are you okay?"

"Me?"

We exchange confused looks. I assume he's embarrassed, so I opt not to say anything about it. He falls back into my arms and we're grinding together when he lets loose again!

"Wes!" I try to laugh, although I'm a little grossed out.

"Dom, it's fine, don't be embarrassed."

"Um, why should *I* be embarrassed?"

He grins. "It's okay. I've heard people fart before. The trackies have farting contests in the locker room all the time."

"Wes!" I sit up and look straight at him. "That wasn't me!"

"Well, it wasn't me."

"Um . . . could it have been Jessica?" I look over at her.

"It sounded like it came from us."

Then it hits me. "Wait, let me try an experiment."

I pull him down against my body and slide a few inches to the right. More flatulence noises! Since the AC is out and we're both dripping with perspiration, it seems that when Wes's chest drags over mine, our sweaty, sticky skin creates these momentary air pockets, which are making those awful sound effects.

"Wow," he says, shaking his head. "That's some kind of cruel physics at work. Do you want to stop?"

Stop? On our last night?

I answer by practically pouncing on him. Soon Wes lightly caresses the sides of my torso, which makes me writhe and arch my back it feels so good. The faux farting continues, but I pretend not to hear, even though it's seriously endangering the ambiance.

A few minutes later I'm the wettest I've ever been, and all I want is for Wes to touch me. I grab both Wes's hands and lead them to my undies. He peels them down slowly, and then reaches between my legs with his right hand. For a few seconds he runs his fingers over my pubic hair, but then without warning he shoves his second finger up my vagina. Or at least he tries to—I don't think he gets farther than a couple inches before I scream out like I've been stabbed.

Jessica leaps up on all fours and starts barking.

Wes jerks his hand away. "Oh, Jesus, Dom, I'm sorry."

I'm silent for a few seconds, trying to dispatch the pain with a few short breaths.

"No, um, don't be sorry," I mumble. "I just wasn't expecting it." I sit up and clutch my stomach. I hope I don't look as annoyed as I am, but that was not fun. I wish he had been gentler.

"I must have gone in at the wrong angle."

"Yeah. Well, no, maybe I'm also just a little tight."

Wes sits at the foot of the bed and holds his head in his hands. "I didn't mean to hurt you. I'm awful."

I have the urge to tell him he's right, but I know that's not fair. I pull up my underwear and say, "Of course I know you didn't mean it." He doesn't move, so after an awkward minute I sit up on my knees and hug him from behind. "Hey, let's take a break from me for a few minutes. Now I just want you to relax."

I push him down on the bed and pull off his boxers. He's completely soft now. Before I have a chance to touch him he pushes my hands away. "Dom, don't worry about it."

I don't get it. Wes let me give him hand jobs both nights last weekend. I think I was actually getting pretty good at it.

"But, Wes, I want to."

"I'm not in the mood," he says like a despondent little boy.

I probably freaked him out when I screamed before. It was so dramatic. I don't know how I could be so stupid.

Then out of nowhere, my stomach starts growling. It sounds like a kitten in the throes of death. How many more terrible noises are we going to have to endure tonight?

"Damn, Dom, is that you?" he asks, lifting his head and smiling incredulously.

"Yeah, I guess I should have eaten something before."

"I'm getting hungry myself. Let's go downstairs. It's cooler there, anyway."

After dressing we head for the kitchen. I'm too shaken up to eat, so I barely get down a slice of toast. Meanwhile, Wes inhales two peanut butter and jelly sandwiches and a whole bag of veggie chips. I don't know how he can have an appetite considering an ocean will be between us this time tomorrow. We're also not speaking; it's as if we've regressed six weeks. My eyes start to water as I imagine this is the beginning of the end. I picture him with Jessica again. Jess and Wes.

After we do the dishes and go back to his bedroom, I summon my sexiest voice and suggest we have another go at it.

"The thing is, Dom, Mom will kill me if I'm not packed by the time they come back. And I still need to walk Jessica."

I'm about to offer to help pack, but rage starts flooding my brain. I don't care if Wes's Paris trip was planned before he met me. If I were him, I would have chosen to stay home and spend my last high school spring break with my girlfriend rather than the old girl next door. It's not like Paris is going anywhere. Wes doesn't even take French!

"Um . . . couldn't you have packed and walked your dog before I came over? You didn't even have practice today. I mean, Wes, this is our last night together for a while."

"I know." He looks down uncomfortably. "But I was reading *Slaughterhouse-Five*." He points to the book on his desk. "I couldn't put it down."

"Oh. In that case . . ." I put my watch and mood ring back on.

"In what case?"

I pull my hair back into a ponytail. "I guess I may as well go now if we're not going to be spending any more quality time together tonight." I get up and slip into my sandals.

"Dom, what are you doing?"

"What does it look like I'm doing?" I grab my purse and turn toward the door. I'm not usually this bitchy, but my behavior feels beyond my control. It's like I can't help being cold to him.

"Dom, I don't get it. What's going on with you?" He follows me downstairs.

I make it as far as the front hallway before I turn around and race back to him. What *is* going on with me? I want to show him I'm unhappy, but not at the expense of driving him away.

"I'm sorry." I stretch out my arms to hug him. "I don't mean to be so awful. It's just that nothing is going the way I wanted tonight. Everything I'm saying and doing is wrong. . . . I don't know, maybe it's just that I'm freaking out about . . . how much I'm going to miss you. . . . And I'm so frickin' sweaty on top of everything."

"Yeah, me too," he says, holding me tightly. "Why don't we do this? Let's give Jessica a quick walk, I'll pack really fast, and then we'll do whatever comes to mind for the rest of the night. My dad has a fan in his den. I'll go get it and put it in my room, all right?"

"Okay." I sniffle. "That sounds great. I'm sorry, Wes."

After we finish with the dog and suitcase, Wes says he needs a few more minutes to straighten up his room. So I sit on the bed and watch him hang up clothes, arrange his books, sort through some papers, and send an e-mail to the EFM track Listserv. Even though I'm waiting for him to turn his attention fully to me, it's almost fun just observing him going about these mundane tasks. It's like every little thing he does is ten times more meaningful than if some other guy were doing it.

When he closes his laptop, Wes spins around on his chair and jumps on top of me. We make out to the soft whirring of the fan for the next two hours. Although he doesn't touch me again down there, he lets me give him two hand jobs, which makes things feel normal again. Every relationship has moments of physical awkwardness, right?

At eleven Wes says his parents are due home at any minute, so we get dressed and walk out to my bike in the backyard.

"Dom, I'm going to miss you a lot. I wish my cell would work in Europe."

"I just wish I wasn't so weird before. I'm really sorry."

"Don't worry about it. . . . We're going to prom, right?"

My eyes widen, surprised. Not exactly the "I love you" I've been waiting for, but almost as good. It certainly makes me feel a lot better about tonight. "Oh, well, I'd love to go, if you want to."

"I only want to if I'm with you."

I smile. "I guess we're going, then." I throw my arms around him. "Thanks so much for asking. I've always wanted to go to a prom."

"Doesn't Shorr have proms?"

I shake my head. "Just lame cotillions in the fall. So this is gonna be my first and only prom."

126

Before I mount my bike, Wes and I have our longest, sweetest kiss to date, and I'm hoping the memory of it will be enough to get me through the next nine days of imagining Wes with Jessica in the City of Lights. And who knows? Maybe absence will make the heart grow fonder. Of course, if my heart grew any fonder, my chest cavity would combust.

20

The following evening the Braffs invite me over to dinner to celebrate Amy's latest triumph. The Fort Myers Museum of Art just asked to display two of her abstract oils! I'm thrilled because being exhibited was always her biggest dream, and until now the only place you could find her work was her house, my house, and EFM's lobby.

The day ends up being a milestone for me as well. It's the first time ever that Amy's stepbrother, Matt, who's home for spring break, says more than "hey" to me. His girlfriend is sitting right next to him, but I swear he does a double take when I enter the dining room.

"Hey, Dom. You look great!"

"Thanks, Matt," I answer nonchalantly as I take my place next to Amy.

After we finish toasting Amy, Dr. Braff grins and says, "Amy tells us you're going steady with Wesley Gershwin."

"Yeah, I guess." I laugh at her dated language. "I'd have brought him but he left this morning for Paris."

"I remember him from Amy's meets," Amy's stepdad says. "Very fast. Good form."

"I didn't know you were dating someone," Matt says quickly, sounding almost disappointed.

I just shrug my shoulders. Amy knowingly nudges me under the table. She has a theory that guys are a lot more attracted to girls with boyfriends than to single girls. I never really understood why, but I suppose it makes sense. Maybe now that I know Wes desires me, I radiate desirability. Come to think of it, I have been looking better these days. I can't remember the last time I was this trim and pimple-free before. My hair and nails seem stronger and shinier. Even Grandma hasn't had to remind me to stand up straight lately.

I still don't have much of an appetite since leaving Wes's yesterday, but Dr. Braff's not offended when I eat only a few forkfuls of the veggie lasagna she made just for me.

She says, "I joke with my therapist friends that if we could bottle lovesickness, it would be the next diet craze."

After we all laugh, Matt says seriously, "You certainly don't need to go on a diet, Dom."

Amy nudges me again, and awkward silence ensues as Matt's girlfriend, who's always been on the chubby side, looks at him disgustedly. I can sense Matt's eyes on me during

129

the rest of the meal, which makes me feel fantastic. Not because I still care for him, but because I couldn't care less.

After dinner Amy and I take a walk on the beach, but we don't get very far before falling down in the sand in paroxysms of shrieks and giggles as I tell her about last night.

"Dom, oh my God!" Amy laughs. "You've been fingered! My innocent little Dom has been fingered!"

"Well, for only, like, two seconds."

"Still. You've been digitally deflowered. A little hokey-*pokey* on the Marvin the Martians!"

"Thanks. Now I'm never gonna think of Looney Tunes the same way again."

"When are you going to go down on him?"

"I don't even know if I could. He's so big."

"Nah. To use medical terminology, just 'say aaaaah.' "

"Amy! It's a penis, not a tongue depressor."

"Good thing you're not vegan or else you wouldn't be allowed to swallow. Semen's an animal product, right?"

"Okay," I laugh, swatting her with my flip-flops. "Now you've gone too far."

We race to the pier, and I gaze up at the stars. It's amazing to think how many millions of people are looking at them right now. I wonder if Wes is. No, he's probably sleeping. Then I look down at the water, the charcoal gray ripples glittering with moonlight. The weather's perfect too, warm with just a slight breeze. If only Wes were here to enjoy this night with me, as well as every other night.

"Earth to Dom, Earth to Dom," Amy teases as we walk back to the beach. "Thinking about Gersh won't bring him home any sooner. And I've been very good about not whining at how little I've been seeing you."

"I'm sorry about that, Ames. But between Wes and keeping up my grades—"

"I know, it's okay. It's preparing me for next year."

I stop short and look back at the pier. "Let's not talk about next year, Ames."

"That's all you would talk about a few months ago."

"Stuff has changed." I etch a heart in the sand with my toes.

"Do you think you and Gersh are going all the way soon?"

"I don't know. I mean, just his finger really hurt."

"It stops hurting. Soon it will feel amazing."

I look around to make sure no one's in earshot. "Um . . . how amazing?"

"My dear Dom." Amy puts her hands on her hips and smiles. "Are you asking me what an orgasm feels like?"

"So what if I am? All I know from class is that it's a bunch of vaginal contractions and a discharge of neuromuscular tensions at the peak of sexual arousal—"

"Only you, Dom, could make Big Os sound like a bad thing."

"And Wes said for guys it feels like Chernobyl."

She laughs. "One of the counselors I hooked up with at camp last summer described it as an H-bomb."

"But what does it feel like for us?"

"It feels . . . you know, wonderful. I'm sorry, it's one of those things that's hard to break down into its components and describe systematically. It's like laughing in that way."

131

"Can't you try?"

"Well, it depends on where you're being stimulated. Some Big Os are more intense than others, more long lasting than others. But it's like there's this little explosion down there, and it radiates through your entire body. More than anything, it's a massive release. And Dom . . ." Amy points to my hands. "You don't need Gersh to get one."

"I guess . . . but I think it'd be more special if I could share it with him."

21

Spring break in the Baylor household is normally uneventful, marked just by a couple of extra visits to Grandma and a few fishing trips. This year my parents insist on occupying every hour of vacation by taking Amy and me out to restaurants, the mall, movies, a baseball game, and the Thomas A. Edison Museum. They don't say it, but I know they're just trying to keep me from sitting around the house freaking out about the approach of Monday, April first—the day most colleges post application status on the Web. Wes has been good about finding Internet cafés in Paris and sending me gushy e-mails. But even though it seems we'll survive spring break without dog-girl wrecking our relationship, what's going to happen come fall?

Judgment Day arrives the same time Wes does. During second period he sends me a text message:

> **Just flew in and checked apps. Fordham no,**
> **but Miami and NYU yes! NYC here I come!**
> **Will be at track till 7. Will pick you up after.**

Of course I'm so curious about my schools I can't concentrate. But I refuse to check at Shorr, where a bunch of the competitive seniors and nosy teachers will pester me about my results, as if it's any of their business. So I hurry home after last period and check on my computer.

Mom's already home since she doesn't teach afternoon classes on Mondays. Dad's home, too, which is unusual—I guess he took off work to be here for this. Ten minutes after I go to my room, my parents knock and ask to come in. They wear the same hopeful, helpless expressions they did the day I received my SAT scores last semester.

After they sit down on the bed, I announce, "Stanford didn't accept me. Didn't even put me on the waiting list."

Dad looks like he's restraining an impulse to kill. "Those assholes!"

My mom glares at him and says to me, "It's their loss, Dommie. California gets earthquake after earthquake, anyway. Your father and I didn't want you living on a fault line."

"As if the hurricanes that hit University of Florida and Tulane are any safer," I mutter, feeling bitchier by the second. "By the way, I got into U of F, like I was expecting."

"Congratulations!" Dad explodes. "That's a damn fine school."

"Oh, congratulations!" Mom parrots. "And that's only four hours away."

"And I got a Distinguished Scholars scholarship to Tulane. That covers about half of tuition."

My mom jumps to her feet. "You were granted a merit scholarship? Oh, Dommie." As she hugs me, Dad's dumbfounded expression transmutes into a grin.

Mom continues, "Do you know how rare and prestigious that is? Tulane's practically rolling out the red carpet for you. And you worked so hard for it. You deserve it."

Then Dad adds, "And all the money left over from your college fund can help pay for med school, if you go."

I unwrap myself from Mom and lay my head on the desk. I've never felt so numb before, but I force my mouth to move. "I'm not going to take the scholarship."

After a beat Dad says, "What? Why not? I thought you wanted to get out of state."

"I do. I want to go to NYU."

Dad thunders, "NYU? When the hell did you apply to NYU?"

My head is still on the desk. "Last minute. In January. I used my Stanford essay and changed a few words. I paid for the application fee with some of my bratsitting money."

"Why the hell didn't you say something, goddamn it?"

"Sweetheart, please," Mom urges Dad.

"Because I didn't think I'd get in. But I did."

"What's wrong with you, Dom?" Dad fumes. "Since when do you go around applying to colleges on the sly? Since we're going to pay for it, don't you think you should have had the crappin' common courtesy to discuss it with us first?"

"Dominique," Mom says reprovingly, "isn't NYU one of the schools Wesley applied to?"

"What?" Dad shouts. "Don't tell me you were dumb enough to apply somewhere because you want to be a groupie to a wishy-washy teenage track putz! You're going to Florida or Tulane, and that's the end of it!"

I lift my head and look at him. I have never seen Dad this angry at me before, and I hate that it has to do with Wes. I start talking softly but gradually intensify to a scream.

"No, Wes isn't the reason behind any of this. New York City is the capital of the world, the school is very prestigious, it has a great premed program, and I'd be stupid to turn down this opportunity. And so what if it costs more? I got in. I got in! You should be happy for me, not yelling at me! And Dad, if you ever say anything bad about Wes from now on, I'll never talk to you again!"

"Dom! Come back here!" Dad bellows behind me as I sprint out of the apartment.

22

I pedal furiously for twenty minutes until I reach my favorite stretch of Fort Myers beach. I throw my bike down on the ground so hard I'm lucky it doesn't break. I'm relieved no one's around except for a few kids too far away to see clearly.

It's chilly out, and there's a light mist in the air. I walk to the edge of the surf and watch the muted sunset, jumping back whenever the waves threaten to lick at my loafers. Then I stretch out on the cool sand and look up overhead, hoping to calm my nerves by watching the clouds glide by, but my mind is spinning.

Just four months ago I *never* would have believed that a boy would play any part whatsoever in my college decision. I cared only about the academics, the size of the student body, the location, and the weather. I used to think of college acceptance letters as emancipation proclamations, but now they're like divorce papers.

I wish I could turn back the clock so I wouldn't have to deal with this mess, with all its variables and uncertainties. Every option seems so costly, and no matter what I choose I'm going to disappoint either my parents or myself. Even going to NYU is no guarantee things will remain as they are now. Maybe Wes doesn't want to have me as a college girlfriend. He never suggested I apply to NYU, and I never told him I did. What will he say? Maybe our relationship won't even survive another day now that we're being forced to consider the future.

The Stanford rejection? It used to be my biggest nightmare. But now I don't care that much. Let's say they did accept me; would I choose Stanford or would I choose NYU? I know what the answer is.

I stand up, run back to the water, and scream at the top of my lungs like a madwoman. I'm so furious at Wes. He single-handedly screwed up my direction and priorities. Because of him, I'm scared of change for the first time in my life. Now, I actually want high school to continue indefinitely. And this is what I've been reduced to. Yelling incoherencies at the Gulf of Mexico.

Soon I'm too out of breath to yell anymore, and I just buckle over and sob. The sand swallows my tears as soon as they hit, as if reassuring me my breakdown will stay secret.

Suddenly my mom's reaction to Tulane runs through my head: *You were granted a merit scholarship? Do you know how rare and prestigious that is?*

My cell phone rings. I lie back on the sand and press TALK.

"Hey, Ames." My voice breaks before I can even get out her name.

"Uh-oh. What's wrong? Was Stanford stupid?"

A half hour later my bike's on the roof of Amy's Camry as she drives me home.

"Thanks for getting me. I don't think I could have pedaled anymore, the way I'm shaking."

"Dom, I don't get it. Why didn't you tell me?"

"I didn't tell anyone. If I didn't get in, then no one would've had to know."

"But why—?"

"Because I wanted to have the option open of being in New York next year, in case something happened between us." My eyes well up again at the thought of being separated.

"When are you going to tell Gersh?"

"I guess I'll have to tonight. He's at stupid track practice for another hour, and I don't know how I'm going to keep it together when he picks me up."

Amy hugs me at the next red light. "Look, I don't want to push you one way or another. The selfish part of me wants you at NYU since it's just a train ride from Amherst. But if you go to Tulane, the money you'll be saving on tuition can buy a lot of plane tickets."

"Yeah. But still."

As Amy pulls up in front of my apartment building, I get another text message, this time from my mom, which makes me choke up again.

We love you and will support whatever decision you make. Just come home. Mom and Dad.

23

"You're going to NYU?" Wes asks quietly. We're on our way to Captiva, and he tightens his grip on the wheel as he responds to my announcement. I can't tell whether he's pleasantly surprised or silently horrified.

"Well, yeah, probably. I can't just end up thirteen hundred miles away from you without putting up a fight." I venture a smile, but Wes is grimacing.

"Did they give you a scholarship too?"

"No, but my parents have already saved enough for tuition, so why not spend it? . . . Are you okay?"

"Yeah, just a little confused. A half ride—well, I'm surprised you'd give that up. I wish I had a scholarship. As it is,

I'm going to have to get part-time work to pay room and board."

I try to ignore his lack of enthusiasm and keep arguing my side. "If I go to Tulane, I'll need to maintain a B-minus to keep my scholarship anyway, and I don't need that added stressor in my life."

"Um, Dom, you'll be able to maintain a B-minus blindfolded, at Tulane or NYU."

"Jesus, Wes!" I glare at him angrily, but all I'm feeling is fear. "Wouldn't you be happy if I went to NYU?"

"Well, yeah. But, Dom, you need to be realistic."

"Oh God," I moan as the tears come and I fall back into my seat. He must think I'm completely obsessed. How could I think it was okay to be this clingy? I turn toward the passenger side window, too hurt and humiliated to face him. "Wes, I can't deal with this now. I don't want . . . I don't think I can handle breaking up tonight. I can't tonight, please?"

"Who said anything about breaking up?" His voice just jumped about two octaves.

"Well, you just said . . ." I look back at him.

"What did I just say? Do *you* want to break up?"

"God, no!" I shout. "Of course I don't want to. Not ever . . ." My words dissolve into more bawling.

Wes veers over to the side of the road, stops the car, and reaches over to hold me. I choke through my tears. "I don't know what's right or what to think."

"Dom . . . this is what I want to say. Whether you go to NYU or Tulane is beside the point because I know you'd do great at either. But I'll feel really guilty if I'm why you turn down this great deal at Tulane. And . . . it just seems that

142

you never would have considered NYU if I weren't in your life."

But you are in my life! Why do you want me to act like you're not?

"Wes, I'm not saying that I'm going to, but if I do go to Tulane . . . do you want to, like, try to keep things the way they are now? I mean, if you find someone you could be potentially interested in, then sure, we'll break things off and still be best friends. We'll always be friends no matter what."

"Dom." Wes laughs while stroking my head. "No one at NYU will compare to you."

I hug him tightly. "You really wouldn't mind doing the distance thing if I went to Tulane?"

"Yeah I'd mind, but I'd deal with it."

"And if I go to NYU, will I, you know, cramp your style? I don't want you to feel like I'm stifling you."

"In a city of eight million people? Don't be ridiculous."

I sit back up in my seat, wipe away the remnants of my tears, and give Wes my best sexy look. "I think we need to relieve some of this tension. How quickly can we get to Captiva?"

I swear the tires leave skid marks, and once we get to the condo, college is the last thing on our minds. Unfortunately, though, neither of us is in the best shape. My nose is stuffed from all the crying I've done today, which makes breathing while kissing tricky. And Wes, just off a transatlantic flight and fresh from track practice, reeks of BO, and his breath is awful. I don't complain, because the only thing that matters is we're together again.

He reaches to pull down my undies, and I lie back next

to him. His left arm is around my shoulders, and his right hand is between my legs. He's much gentler and slower than last time. But as he bobs in and out of me, I don't really feel anything. Soon he thumbs my clitoris simultaneously, which feels . . . okay. I fake some moaning noises every few seconds so he'll keep going, but I wouldn't say I'm enjoying it. If an orgasm doesn't feel much better than this, I don't know what all the hoopla is about. I can tell Wes is getting discouraged.

After ten minutes of nothing, I say, "You can stop now. I absolutely love this, Wes, but I just need to relax more."

"I want to make you come."

"You will. Let's just rest awhile. I'm sure I'm just too emotional right now to get into it."

"All right," he sighs, resting his head on my chest. "Oh, I forgot to tell you. My mom made an appointment at Charles's Formal Wear next week. Prom will be the first time I ever wear a tux."

"Well, prom will be the first time I ever wear an evening gown. I bought mine at the mall last week."

"Cool. Can't wait to see you in it . . . and not in it."

I playfully pinch his arm. "Mom thought it was so pretty that she made me bring it to Grandma's to try it on for her. I was expecting her to shoot me down like she always does, but she actually liked it. It was great seeing her satisfied for once. Then she started reminiscing about going to her prom with Grandpa and wearing her white lace prom dress. And she was showing me old pictures, and, um, I couldn't help but think of all the . . . traditions that go with prom."

"Yeah. Like slow-dancing. I hate slow-dancing."

"Me too. But what I meant was prom *night,* you know?"

"I think so." He gulps through his grin.

"I mean, only if we're both ready. Prom's still a whole month away."

"Oh, I'm ready. You're sure you are?" He lifts his head up and looks at me hopefully.

I smile at his enthusiasm. Then I shut my eyes as I hear my grandma's grating voice warning me to abstain until marriage. I don't think that's bad advice. But I want to have sex when the time is right *for me,* and how could it feel more right than with Wes, at his prom? The only thing making me hesitate is we haven't said "I love you" yet. But really, what's the point of declaring it when we imply it every day?

I open my eyes and nod at him. "I just want to be as physically close to you as I possibly can, you know? I want nothing separating us."

"I guess I should go buy some condoms."

"Way ahead of you," I giggle as I reach into my purse. "I took a trip to CVS this week. I thought maybe we could practice putting it on."

Wes looks at me in awe, and he gets hard again just by studying the box and reading the instructions. After tearing off the wrapper, Wes holds the condom about a half inch away from the head of his penis. Then he pinches the tip of the condom to get the excess air out, and with the other hand he rolls it all the way down.

"Wow, Wes, you really seem to know what you're doing."

"I had a lot of practice in Paris."

"What did you say?"

"April Fools'!"

I'm laughing and wheezing at the same time. "You know . . ." I peel off the condom and slap him on his arm with it. "So *not* funny!"

He laughs. "In health class they made us practice putting these on dildos. I just never knew it'd come in handy so soon."

I shake my head as I search my purse for a tissue to put the condom in. It looks like Saran Wrap. It feels like it too, except a little thicker. And slimier. It's mind-boggling to think this flimsy-looking apparatus is going to be inside me, that it's the only thing between me and pregnancy.

Meanwhile, Wes is rubbing his forehead with his fingers. He looks exhausted.

"You okay?"

"Yeah," he breathes. "It's just been a crazy day."

"Yeah, I know, right? Intercontinental travel, college acceptances, a little third base, and now condom dry runs."

"It's enough to wear a guy out." He closes his eyes and settles into the pillow. Then he says drowsily, as if he were reading my mind, "I want our first time to be incredible, Dom."

I turn on my side to hold him as he falls asleep. I lie awake admiring his perfect face and body until it's time to go home.

24

Seven different guys ask Amy to prom this year, but she ends up asking Wes's friend Paul so she can throw "the most kick-ass after-party EFM's ever seen" at his beach house. I tell my parents I'm helping her with the cleanup and will probably spend the night at her place since it will be late by the time we're done. They say that's fine and that they just want me to have a good time. They even offer to treat me to a spa day beforehand. I hate how parents whip out their best, most generous qualities right before you have to lie to them.

Prom morning, I ask Mom if I can borrow the station

wagon so I can go to the mall to buy panty hose and makeup. Instead, I drive all the way out to the Sanibel Regal Resort, where I have already reserved a small room with a view of the beach. Wes's grandparents are in Captiva now for a two-week vacation, but I'm actually glad we can't use their condo tonight. I don't want our first time to be in a place where we have to worry about leaving it without a trace, even though the hotel room is costing Wes a month's allowance money and me most of my bratsitting earnings.

After checking in, I go up to the room and stash my toiletries and a change of clothes so I'll have something casual to wear tomorrow morning. In the nightstand drawer I drop in a package of extra-strength condoms and a lubricant Amy read about that's supposed to make sex less painful the first time. Finally I drive to the spa where I get a full-body massage, trying not to think how I have to make my final college decision by next week.

Wes and I actually haven't seen each other in six days since he's been away in Tallahassee for the state track championship. So even though I'm dying to hug him when the doorbell rings at five sharp, I have my parents stall for a few minutes so I can make a fashionably late grand entrance into the living room.

We both bust up laughing when we lay eyes on each other. Wes looks so distinguished in a tux and bow tie, and he has never seen me look this glamorous. My form-fitting gown is dark green silk strewn with tiny rhinestones, and spaghetti straps cross the low-cut back. Topping off the ensemble is Grandma's emerald ring, which Grandpa had given her on their first wedding anniversary and which she's lending me for the night. It was strange taking off Wes's mood ring today since I've been wearing it almost nonstop for the last two months, but admittedly it's not prom material.

When we stop giggling, all Wes manages to say is, "Wow!"

I pin a red rose boutonniere on his lapel, and the roses in the corsage he slips on my wrist are yellow except for the tips of the petals, which are red. It's perfect since yellow signifies friendship and red means romance, and we have both.

Dad breaks out his digicam and takes almost a hundred photographs of us striking poses in the living room and on our terrace. Normally, Wes's smile rarely exceeds a tight-lipped grin, but tonight it's ear to ear. On the elevator ride down to the parking lot he says his cheeks hurt from smiling so much.

Unfortunately, prom is anticlimactic after our romantic four-course candlelit dinner at The Kings Crown. The dance is supposed to have an outer space theme, but the EFM gymnasium looks less like the Moon and more like where black and silver crepe paper goes to die. When I use the restroom I notice a Marvin the Martian poster next to the tampon dispenser, which reminds me of Wes's bedsheets. For a second I wonder if the prom committee knows tonight's the night and did that to tease me. I also feel a little lost since Amy's the only other EFM-er I know well, and she and Paul leave early to prepare for the after-party.

After we get professional pictures taken against a kitschy backdrop of a little green man and a tinfoil rocketship, Wes says to me, "So, uh, I think this is the part where I ask you to dance?"

"Your enthusiasm is overwhelming," I tease. "It's okay, I know you don't like dancing."

"So what?" He offers me his arm. "It's prom."

I've actually been dreading this moment because I hate the way people slow-dance today. I wish we were still taught real dances, like the waltz or swing, so we could look coordinated and graceful. Instead, couples just sway back and forth and lurch in an awkward circle as we girls stiffly grip the guys' shoulders and the guys cup our waists in a display of mutual rigor mortis. Amy calls this the Dance of the Dying Cockroach.

But slow-dancing with Wes exceeds all expectations. On the dance floor he holds me so close I can rest my head on his chest, which makes the obligatory swaying actually feel really sensual. Occasionally he eases his fingers under the straps of my dress and strokes my lower back, which turns me on so much it takes all my self-control not to grab his ass and grind up against him. I love that people are looking at us, wondering who that lucky girl is.

We spend two hours at Amy's after-party, which is longer than we planned. I think we're both nervous about tonight and are trying to delay the inevitable, but we're also having a fantastic time. Amy and Paul brought in two dozen cakes from The Bubble Room. They also set up Dance Dance Revolution and karaoke, and it's hilarious watching all the drunk EFM-ers attempt to dance to the beat and rap in time with the music. But when one of the girls starts belting out Donna Summer's "Dim All the Lights," Wes and I both start to get antsy.

I ask Wes to get the car and pick me up in front of Paul's house so I won't have to walk the five blocks in my heels.

Meanwhile, I find Amy to say goodbye. As we hug she whispers, "Don't get discouraged if tonight's no good. Doing it for the first time rarely is for the girl. And remember you don't have to go through with it. You can always change your mind at the last second."

"I know, I know. I won't do anything I don't want to." I'm still stunned I'm about to go further than Amy ever has. I guess she is too since her eyes are starting to overflow.

"Oh, Ames, don't."

"I'm sorry," she laughs through her tears. "I just can't believe how fast the time's gone, you know? It's almost May."

"I can't believe it either." Suddenly the prospect of having sex seems almost like a death sentence for the person I've been all my life up until this night. A part of me wishes I could be an innocent brace-faced freshman again, just for a few minutes, anyway.

"Now don't you start crying either," Amy admonishes me while dabbing her eyes. "You've got a long night of bronco riding ahead of you, cowgirl."

I sniffle and grin. "Way to kill a tender moment."

"You know I'm hopeless," she says, shaking her head in mock shame.

We hug again before I leave to walk down the beach and up the wooden staircase to the street. As I come over the dune, I see Wes is already waiting, his eyes and the Explorer glowing the same neon blue in the moonlight.

"Hey," he says.

"Hey."

25

We start going at it in the tiny hallway of our hotel room. Within seconds my lipstick is all over Wes's face, and I have to order him to stop for a minute so we can delicately take off and hang up our expensive outfits—the last clothes we'll wear as virgins. As soon as I close the closet doors he lifts me up high over his head, carries me to the bed, and throws me on it. We're both laughing, but I'm amazed to see him this brazen and aggressive. I remember one of the first things I wondered about him the day we met was if he could bench me. I guess he can.

I spot the chocolates the maid left on our pillows. After

popping one in my mouth, I pierce the outer shell with my teeth and let the runny hazelnut filling wash over my tongue.

"Kith shme," I say.

He looks at me askance.

"Pleeeeshe?" I give him puppy eyes.

"All right. Why not?"

And it tastes so good. It gets all over our chins and drips onto our chests. Some dribbles onto my breasts, and Wes tries licking it off, only to get us both dirtier. I wonder if all couples get this kinky this fast.

"That is the only way to eat chocolate," Wes says. "I think we're going to have to shower together."

"Oh yeah?"

"Uh-huh. But later."

Wes climbs on top of me. We're kissing almost brutally with our tongues and teeth, sucking each other's lips and chins as we grab at each other's torsos with clenched fingers. Then I mutter through my kisses that the stuff is in the nightstand.

Wes sits up, opens the drawer, rips open a condom, and rolls it on quickly even though his hands are shaking. When he gets back on top of me, I feel some of the lube he coated the condom with rubbing off on my thighs. I wrap my legs around him and raise my hips, but he doesn't move.

"This is the point where I was hoping my masculine animal instincts would kick in."

"This all feels fine so far. You know, normal."

"Dom, I'm really scared this is going to be painful for you."

I am too, but more than that I'm excited. "I'm sure all

the, you know, fingering stuff we've been doing already kinda broke me in. I'll tell you if it hurts."

"Okay," he says warily.

"Hey, Wes, are you having any doubts about this?"

"No, are you?"

"No. This feels so right to me."

"I love you, Dom."

There, the final piece of the jigsaw.

He shakes his head. "It's insane how much I love you. I never knew I could feel this way."

"I love you too," I say quietly, holding back my tears. It feels *so* good to have said it, finally, and to be this honest and exposed. It's like I've discovered the meaning of life—to love and be loved. Sure, my parents and I love each other, but we have no choice. We're family. Love seems so much more special when it comes from someone who has no obligation to feel it.

The next few seconds are pretty awkward as I try to reposition my pelvis to accommodate his angle, and Wes is careful not to put excessive weight on me. Finally, I feel him enter me slightly.

"Yeah, it's fine," I say. "It doesn't hurt."

"Okay." He slowly eases in a little more. It doesn't feel that much different than if it were his index and middle fingers. But then he shoves into me at full force.

"Ow! Get off!" I shout.

He jumps off the bed. "Oh crap, I'm sorry."

"No, don't be," I say as I curl up in the fetal position. "I'm sorry I yelled."

"Shit, did I hurt you bad?"

Yeah, it hurt like hell.

"Just a little."

I turn on the nightstand lamp and pull the blanket up over my knees to shield my lower body from Wes's view. I don't see any blood on the sheets, but there are a couple of red drops on my inner thighs. I smear them away with my fingers and sink back into the pillow. Then Wes lies down next to me. We are silent for a minute.

"Wes, we just had sex." I laugh and groan at the same time.

"Well, it was kinda crummy."

"It wasn't crummy! The first time is supposed to be weird—if it were great on the first try, we'd have nothing to aim for later."

"Uh . . . you want to try again?"

I do, but I also want to wash off my heavy prom makeup and remove all the bobby pins from my hair, so I tell Wes I'll just be a few minutes in the bathroom.

Once there, I let the faucet run and study myself in the mirror. I'm not sure what to think. My body doesn't feel any different. I gaze down at my arms and stomach and legs, and I don't look any different. But I am different. I just had sex. My vagina had a penis inside of it. I wonder if my Shorr friends and teachers will detect it somehow, or my mom and dad for that matter. It's going to feel so weird being sexually active, living in the same apartment with the two people who had to have sex to create me.

I turn the water on higher as I cry a little. A part of me does feel like I've just lost something precious—I think of Grandma equating virginity with a white wedding dress, and I wonder if Wes will be the one I marry. He has to be. Who else could it be? I bet Wes would be a great dad one day, very hands-on and loving. His parents would be fantastic grandparents too. I imagine them in their pastel sweatsuits babysitting, giving our kids piggyback rides and showing them how to build with blocks.

I take my Grandma's emerald ring off my right hand and put it on my left ring finger for a minute. As I hold out my hand and admire it, I think how funny it is that of all the people I know, I—little Miss Science Quiz priss—am the least likely to have lost it on prom night, with a state champion sprinter jock, of all people.

After peeing, washing my face, and brushing out my hair-sprayed hair, I crawl back into bed with a sleeping Wes. I kiss him on the mouth until he awakens.

"You were really out," I say once he opens his eyes.

"It's no surprise." He yawns. "I ran harder in the last week than I have all semester. My legs are so sore I can't feel my feet."

"Oh, really? Well, that means you won't be bothered if . . . *I tickle them!*"

Before I get a chance to tickle anything, Wes whizzes up, seizes my wrists, and throws me down on the bed. Soon we are having sex again, but this time he is moving in and out very, very slowly. We're able to go for a full two minutes before I tell him to stop because I'm too sore down there but that we can try again in the morning.

It's three a.m. at this point. We call the concierge and order a ten a.m. wake-up call since checkout's at noon. Then we pull the blankets up over us and lie quietly in each other's arms. Our first whole night together.

We're about to drift off when Wes holds me tighter and says groggily, "Just so you know, this has been the best day of my life."

And it was mine too.

PART III

26

Subject: ☹
Date: Monday, August 19, 6:50 p.m.

Dear Dom,

Just finished my last day at the library. All in all it was a good summer gig, but I can't wait to get out of Fort Myers, which feels like a ghost town now that you're en route to Tulane. First thing I'll unpack in New York is my awesome new cologne! I showed it to my parents this morning, and they love the smell too. I should have thought to get you a going-away gift also, but I'm bad when it comes to those things. I wish you had something besides a cheap mood ring to remember me by.

Some good news. I talked to the people at student employment today, and they're going to let me lifeguard at NYU's pool! I'm relieved I didn't end up with a cafeteria job.

Missing you, Wes

Subject: ☺
Date: Tuesday, August 20, 9:46 p.m.

Hey boyfriend,

Greetings from the Big Easy! I just tracked your flight on my laptop, and in only two hours you'll be in the Big Apple! A huge part of me wishes I were sitting in the seat next to you, planning and plotting our four-year NYC adventure, but there's no need to get into all of that again. This was the most practical, logical decision, and I'm excited about what's next.

I guess you can say I survived the drive over, but being confined for thirteen hours with Mom and Dad in the car was trying. Whenever I got sad, though, all I had to do was hold my mood ring, which I *love* btw, and I felt better. ☺

Tonight we're crashing at a bed-and-breakfast in the French Quarter. I want to stay up until you land, but I better get to sleep since tomorrow we're waking up at the crack of dawn to beat the dorm move-in rush. I'm counting down the days until Thanksgiving break (99) and Xmas break (121). Yuck. Write or call me soon!!!!!!! I love you, Dom

P.S. It's weird to be e-mailing you again after all these months! But that's how it all started, eh? ;-)

P.P.S. Congrats on the lifeguard job! I had no idea you were even certified! You see? Even after all this time I'm still learning new things about you.

Subject: NYU, baby! (note my new e-mail address)
Date: Wednesday, August 21, 2:35 p.m.

Hey Dom,

It's great to be back in the City, although I had no idea how much I'd gotten used to the quiet of Florida. Last night after my grandparents took me back to their loft, I kept waking up to every car alarm and ambulance siren.

Jess and one of her French major friends helped me move in this morning. I brought only four suitcases, so I was unpacked in less than an hour. My roommate, Gerard, is from Ghana (Africa)! I thought *I* had a long plane ride. He's a good guy, plans to major in theater. He saw our prom pic on my desk and said in his Ghanaian accent (which almost sounds French), "Whoa, she's beautiful, man." I told him not to get any ideas. ;-)

I'm going to the campus store now to pick up a few things.

I love you, W

P.S. I'll call you tonight after our hall meeting.

Subject: Tulane so far
Date: Thursday, August 22, 9:45 p.m.

Dear Ames,

Forgive the e-mail but I have only a couple hundred minutes left, and I want to use them sparingly until they get replenished Sept. 1.

I can't believe we're actually in college! It's finally happening! My roommate, Caitlin, moved in last night, and not to jinx it, but she seems very sweet and considerate. She even offered to stay with Chapin, her boyfriend of FOUR YEARS and a junior here, whenever Wes visits! Chapin is six five, and Caitlin's only five feet, so they're a funny-looking couple, but they're really into

163

each other. He plays cello and she plays viola, and they met in orchestra at their high school in Baton Rouge.

As for Tulane itself, I'm feeling good. I'm a little envious of Caitlin for having her bf with her, but I'm also afraid Tulane will just be a continuation of high school for her rather than a new experience. Don't get me wrong. I'm thinking about Wes 24/7. Most of all, I'm still really humiliated about how I screwed up on Sunday at Captiva. My head was literally down there, Ames. I was hovering over it, but for some reason I just couldn't bring myself to take it in my mouth. What's crazy is that it should have been a breeze. I mean, we've made love 32 times since prom! I know Wes said it was fine I wasn't ready yet, but it was our last night together, and I wanted everything to be perfect.

On top of everything, Wes already saw the dog-girl, and he's going to be a campus lifeguard! I spent all summer paranoid about the Southwest Florida College girls flirting with him at the library, and now I hate the NYU swim team and am wishing dog-girl drops out of Columbia and goes back to Texas. I feel so weird hating someone I've never even met before. Oh, and my parents gave me the trillionth "You're too young to be serious so keep your eyes open and embrace your surroundings" speech. Ugh!

I don't mean to sound sad, it's just Wes Withdrawal. Besides that I'm really pumped. Anyway, how's New England treating you? Any new notches on your bedpost? Or should I say cotpost?

I miss you very much, Dom

Subject: Thank you for your help!
Date: Friday, August 23, 2:44 p.m.
Dear Mom (please read to Dad too),

I just wanted to write and thank you both for helping me move in, you esp., Dad, for taking off work. You'll be glad to know

I registered for bio and chem today. I'm determined to give premed a fair shot even though I'm still on the fence about it. If it doesn't work out, I'll just major in something fun, like glass blowing with a minor in ballroom dance. Just kidding! But they really do offer those classes here!

I've met a ton of new people in the last couple of days. Overall everyone's really nice, except there's this one spoiled brat on my hall who's never used a washing machine before(!!), let alone a communal one, and she's disgusted she has to share a hall bathroom with us. Four other girls on my hall already requested roommate changes! People can be so catty.

Anyway, I have yet another orientation meeting to go to, so I better get going. Say hi to Grandma too. I'll call her when I'm a little more settled in. Talk to you soon.

Love, Dom

Subject: WE'RE COLLEGE GIRLS NOW!!!
Date: Friday, August 23, 3:15 p.m.

Dear Dom,

I'm writing this from Amherst's fine arts building. I just found out we're gonna have nude male models in our drawing class! To quote Little Orphan Annie, I think I'm gonna like it here. ☺

That's hilarious about Chapin and Caitlin's height difference. I wonder how they 69. My roommate, Soo May, seems really nice too and plans to major in computer science. She's lived in Massachusetts all her life, but her family's Malaysian.

I wouldn't worry about Gersh being a lifeguard. I'm sure he'll take the job just as seriously as he did track and won't goof around. If you're still concerned, send a letter to the NYU swim team saying Gersh has a New Orleans girlfriend who's learning voodoo and is not afraid to use it! But seriously, you spent all of

April doing the pro-con thing with both schools, and I still think you made the right decision.

I also wouldn't worry about the non–blow job. Believe me, it could've been A LOT worse. The first time I went down on a guy I was *too* into it and almost bit it off! What I *would* be worried about is your non–Big O. It's just not fair he's the only one who's been getting off. I know your excuse—"just loving Wes is orgasm enough." Well, whatever makes you happy, but you can't be afraid to lose control and let your body go.

But on to the big news of the week: I've hooked up with only 1 guy so far! Joel lives in my dorm, he's going to be a fine arts major too, his bod's totally ripped, and he's from Kansas, which makes sense since he can do the tornado with his tongue. :P~ Last night we hardly hooked up at all! We just talked and talked. I never thought I'd be pairing off with someone this soon in this buffet of Amherst guys, but I really like him. Maybe soon we'll both be nonvirgins!

Your best friend always who misses you terribly, Amy

Subject: Miss you
Date: Friday, August 23, 11:56 p.m.
Hey Dom,

There's a huge party going on down at the NYU Student Center right now, and here I am, sitting in my room like the wuss I am. You'd think after moving so much as a kid, I'd be a pro at meeting new people. But I'm just so tired of it. Maybe I'm also just nervous about this semester. I've been looking over the syllabi for my classes next week, and, Dom, I've never been assigned so much reading in my life. Who knows how I'll be able to do track next semester?

I also really miss Jessica. She's been with me forever, and now that she's older and can barely move around, I'm gone when she needs me the most.

Hmmm . . . just writing you has made me feel better about everything. ☺ I think I'll go out to that party after all. W

Subject: I love you!!
Date: Saturday, August 24, 2:04 a.m.

Oh sweetie!! I just called your cell and got vm, so I'm assuming you're still out partying.

It's totally normal to feel out of place and nervous about classes. In a few weeks you'll be completely adjusted. I'm also sorry you're missing Jessica and that her arthritis is getting worse, but I'm sure your parents are taking good care of her. You know, "missing" seems to be the theme of this week. By my count, 6 of the 22 girls on my hall have long-distance boyfriends too. It's nice to know I'm not alone, but one of the girls, Julia, is in an "open" relationship. I mean, that's the most ridiculous thing I've ever heard! She claims she loves and misses her "boyfriend," yet she's already screwed one of the guys on the third floor! Just the thought of even looking at another guy makes me want to hurl. I'm not kidding.

What else? Oh, I don't remember if I told you that our room's on the tenth floor, which is the top, so we have one of the best views on campus! I can't wait to show you in person, but until then, attached is a JPEG.

Love you always, kisses, and more kisses, Dom

P.S. Btw, Amy's loving Amherst, and it looks like she may be dating someone for real! I know, hell just froze over. I just hope he makes her as happy as you make me. ☺

Subject: We miss our little girl!

Date: Saturday, August 24, 8:04 a.m.

Dear Dommie,

Thank you for your sweet e-mail. We got in late last night, and we continue to be impressed by how well the station wagon is holding up. It's hard to believe it's been seventeen years since we bought it. It's also hard to believe it's been seventeen years since you came into our lives. It was our pleasure to help you move in, and it is our joy to watch you embark on this next chapter of your life. I don't know if you noticed, but your father got misty-eyed during the president's convocation speech yesterday morning. We're both so proud of you.

It's going to be sad to start a new year at Shorr on Monday without my Dommie there, and our weekly excursions to Grandma will feel incomplete without your presence. Try to send her a postcard if you can. I know she's always looking for things to display on her fridge. I don't think she's added anything new since your beautiful prom pictures.

We miss you and are looking forward to Thanksgiving.

Love, your empty nester mother

27

It's seven weeks into school when the roof caves in. Literally. I'm in a deep sleep, but my eyes fly open at five forty-five a.m. to water splattering against my forehead and the sound of thunder directly overhead. The bottom half of my blanket is drenched, and before I can process what's happening I hear Caitlin yell, "What the fuck?" We both leap out of bed and are horrified to find ourselves splashing around in an inch of rainwater.

"Oh shit!" we scream in unison as I grab my flashlight, which Dad bought for me to keep by my bed in case of blackouts. I switch it on and point it to the ceiling, revealing a massive brown water mark. The top layer of paint is creased and hanging in jagged pieces, and water's dripping down through a million tiny cracks. Our dorm room is raining.

"Fuck! Fuck!" I keep screaming as I plod to my closet and take out trash bags to drape over our computers and her viola case. As Caitlin starts picking up our shoes and moving them to higher ground, it occurs to me to get our RA, so I slosh into the hall and knock on Meagan's door. She must see the panic on my face because she runs into our room before I can even explain.

"Holy shit!" she shouts.

The three of us just stand there for a few seconds, our mouths agape at the surreal scene, before Meagan springs into action and phones the Res-Life director. After assuring us an emergency crew is on its way, she unlocks the janitor's closet and drags in six empty trash cans, which we position under the heaviest leaks. The workmen are here just twenty minutes later, but it takes them the next four hours to plug up the ceiling and vacuum out the water. In the meantime, Meagan lends Caitlin and me her futon, but I'm too on edge to sleep. I just lie there cold and wet, thinking how sunnier weather was one of the pros I put in the Tulane column and not in the NYU column.

We're finally allowed back in the room later that morning, and it's a disaster area. The carpet's a marsh, the smell is noxious, Caitlin's stack of sheet music is indecipherable, my Herophilus poster is ripped and crinkled, and my biology textbook, which I had left on the floor open to the chapter I was studying last night, is so saturated the pages are completely glued together. Luckily, our clothes are dryly tucked away in dresser drawers and the recessed closets. Most of all, I'm just grateful my prom photos are protected in frames.

Our alarm clocks aren't running, since the workmen had to shut off our electricity, so I don't realize I'm late for biology until I find my water-resistant Seiko under the bed, where it floated away overnight. Meagan advises us to skip classes today and offers to treat us to breakfast on Res-Life's dime, but I'm too nervous about getting behind in my notes.

When I finally make it there forty minutes late, the professor looks down at his seating chart and points at me.

"Ms. Baylor, you know I count tardiness as an absence. And you're allowed only one absence before I mark down your grade."

"I know, I'm so sorry, there was a floo—"

"I don't need to hear excuses. Robin has your midterm," he says, motioning to our TA in the front row.

My face feels as red as my hair. Nothing like this ever happened to me back at Shorr. I walk hurriedly toward Robin, my head bowed in mortification. When I reach his desk, he looks at me blankly and drops the paper in my hands. At the top in a big red circle is my grade. Seventy-two.

My jaw drops. This is the first C of my life. I thought Shorr was supposed to prepare me for college-level work. Oh my God! My scholarship. I need to keep a 2.7 GPA for my scholarship.

"Is there a problem, Ms. Baylor?" the professor asks flatly.

Startled out of my trance, I whip around and realize everyone is staring at me. I scurry to my seat and fight back tears the rest of the class, trying not to think how the scholarship was Tulane's biggest pro. Later in lab, I accidentally contaminate my tissue cultures and have to redo the entire experiment. Thank God it's Friday.

When I finally get back to my room that evening, Caitlin's packing a duffel bag.

"Are you going to Chapin's?" I ask weakly.

"So are you. Meagan said the workmen will need all weekend to fix the roof and plaster and paint this sardine can. We gotta be outta here by tonight and can't come back till Monday. So get your stuff together."

I rub my temples with my hand, too weary even to speak all the four-letter words I'm thinking. "Okay. Thanks, Caitlin." I muster up enough energy to wrench my suitcase out of the cramped cinder-block closet, and I think how awesome it would be if I were packing for my boyfriend's place rather than my roommate's boyfriend's place. I perk up. Of course! I have plenty of money for plane fare from working for Amy's mom this summer, and this weekend's Columbus Day. Wes and I had decided to try to stick it out until we saw each other over Thanksgiving, but why suffer? Could this curse be a blessing in disguise?

I pull my laptop from its protective trash bag, and I have just enough battery strength left to send out an SOS.

Subject: Shipwrecked!
Date: Friday, October 11, 6:30 p.m.
Ahoy Captain Wes,
This is my message in a bottle. My room has capsized (flooded with rainwater), and Caitlin and I are abandoning ship. They're

forecasting storms all weekend, and I have nowhere to dock. Can you offer me a dry, comfy harbor? New York has a great (air)port! ☺

Your first mate, Dom

Sure, it's a little cheesy, but I know Wes will think it's cute. After I press SEND, I leap up and start thinking about what I should pack for a weekend in the Big Apple. That's when the fire alarm sounds.

28

"Oh God," I wail over the siren as I press my hands to my ears. "What next?"

"As if anything could burn in this bog," Caitlin shouts as she grabs her umbrella.

I sling my knapsack over my shoulder, and we file down all ten flights of stairs with a hundred other disgruntled freshmen. When we get to the lobby, Caitlin tells me she's going to dash across campus to Chapin's, and after his Sigma Nu meeting they'll drive his pickup truck back here to get me and our luggage.

In the meantime, I scout out a dry patch of pavement

under the awning of the dorm's back entrance. I sit down cross-legged, take out my books, and try to study while the firemen take their time checking all the rooms.

A few minutes later I hear, "Hey, little lady. Aren't fire drills annoying?"

Wincing at the hokey pick-up line, I mumble, "Hey" without bothering to see who the guy is. I've been hit on a couple times since school started, and I learned that if I don't react, boys quickly lose interest and go away.

"Studying hard?"

I don't respond.

"You have a white streak on your hair. You look like a redheaded Cruella De Vil."

"Excuse me?" I shoot back, finally looking up at him.

He's about five foot nine, stocky, and not especially cute. He has curly, mousy brown hair that matches his eyes, and he's wearing the archetypal male student wardrobe of plaid boxer shorts, a Tulane sweatshirt, a baseball cap, and Birkenstock sandals. He clearly hasn't shaved in a couple of days.

"Your hair." He gestures. "There's a white stripe on top."

He reaches out to touch my head but I instinctively slap his hand before he makes contact.

"Ouch, woman!" He recoils.

"Sorry, but you invaded my comfort zone." Hitting him may have been a little much, but I've had a nightmarish day, after all.

"Damn, you *are* Cruella De Vil." He massages his knuckles. "I was just going to remove it for you."

I pat my hair with my hand and peel off what looks like a chalky white strip of paper. "Oh. Um, there's a leak in my room and the paint's coming down. Some of it must have just fallen on me. No biggie." I look down at my textbook again.

"That was your room? Man, that sucks. Don't worry, though. Res-Life's quick about fixing this kind of stuff. I'm the RA on the sixth floor, so I know these things."

I want to say that banishing Caitlin and me from our room all weekend long isn't "quick," but it's not worth my energy.

After a silence he says, "So, are you going to introduce yourself? Or should I continue calling you Cruella?"

"Listen." I glare at him. "I don't mean to be bitchy, but I have tons of work and I'd appreciate it if you let me study."

"You'll hurt your eyes. There isn't much light back here."

"I'll be fine." I focus on the page and pretend to read.

He seizes my textbook from my lap.

"Hey, give that back!" I stand up and shift my gaze from the book to his hopeful face. He smiles, obviously unaware he's being a creep.

"I first saw you during orientation, and since then I've been working up the courage to speak to you. I finally have it, so give me a break, all right?"

I look away in response, taken aback by his candor. Then he continues, "So I'll start. Hi, I'm Calvin Brandon."

I sigh before murmuring, "Hey. I'm Dominique."

"That's more like it. So, let's see, what are you studying? Ah. Chemistry. Let me guess. Premed?"

"Maybe."

He hands my book back to me. "I started as premed

myself, but it was way out of my league. Now I'm a double in econ and poly sci, with a minor in French."

I want to say I couldn't care less about those subjects, especially the French.

"So, where are you from?" he persists.

I sigh again before answering.

"Florida?" His eyes widen. "That's nice and warm. I'm from Chicago."

"So?"

"I see we took our happy pill today, Cruella. Are you at least excited for the freshman semiformal tomorrow?"

"One, I already told you my name is Dominique. And two, I don't think I'll be going."

"You gotta! We have a great DJ who plays all the eighties classics. And this year The Gumbo Shop's catering. Personally, I can't wait. Why wouldn't you go?"

Because I'm going to be with my studly track star boyfriend in New York City!

I ask him, "Why would *you* be going to a freshman dance? If you're an RA, you must be a junior or senior."

"Junior, and it's precisely *because* I'm an RA. I have to be there to chaperone . . . and dance with you."

"I don't like to dance."

As if answering my prayers, the firemen give the all clear.

"Okay, Calvin, see you around," I say mechanically as I put away my textbook. I'm anxious to resume my packing upstairs.

"Not so fast."

Calvin actually digs his hand into my knapsack and fishes out my cell phone.

"Hey!" I'm raising my voice at him. "What gives you the right?"

"Just one second. . . ." He punches some buttons. "There. Now you have my number. Don't be afraid to call it."

I don't answer or even look at him as I grab my phone and dart into the building. Being on the receiving end of some tool's unabashed flirtations while I'm missing Wes so desperately is nauseating—like being force-fed milkshakes when all I want is a glass of water. I call Wes and leave a voice mail.

29

That night I lie on Chapin's futon gripping my cell phone in both hands. Wes and I have been talking every two or three days since we started school, but it's the weekend now and we haven't spoken since Monday. Why hasn't he gotten back to me?

Could he have had an accident? Maybe his phone's broken and his Internet's down. Is he having sex with Jessica? *Stop doubting him, Dom!* I can't start living in a constant state of paranoia, not with four long years of distance still ahead of us.

When Amy calls me around midnight I seriously consider not answering. The last thing I want to hear about right now is her storybook romance with Joel and all the mind-blowing sex they're having. But I know Amy would never deliberately dodge my calls, so I begrudgingly click TALK. After I fill her in on the leak, she says I'm welcome to fly out to Amherst and stay with her and Soo May if New York doesn't work out. I wish boyfriends could be as reliable as best friends. After leaving Wes a second voice mail, I drift off to sleep trying to tune out the sound of Caitlin and Chapin screwing in the next room. Apparently, Caitlin has no trouble reaching the Big O.

The next night, Saturday, Caitlin jumps on my futon and pulls my arms until I finally agree to go to the freshman semi with her and Chapin. I'm in no mood to party, but it's something to do besides waiting for my cell to ring. Surely he's received my desperate messages by now. Or has he?

While Caitlin and Chapin are getting dressed in his room, I Google Wes's name on my laptop. I'm half-hoping and half-afraid I'll come across bad news, such as NYU FROSH FOUND DEAD. CONTACT WITH LOVED ONES UNSUCCESSFUL. But all I find are old Fort Myers *Tribune* articles reporting his track scores. The pathetic thing is, reading them actually makes me feel closer to him.

Next I check Amazon.com, where he keeps a long wish list of books. It says he added three new novels today, so I'm relieved he's probably okay . . . but how can he think about literature when he knows I've been trying to reach him?

I sigh as I turn off the computer and open my suitcase. I step into my black halter-top slip dress, which I wore to Wes's graduation dinner four and a half months ago and which I had packed in the hope of sporting it at some hip

SoHo restaurant with him this weekend. But after I pull up the back zipper, I'm startled to find that the skirt section rides up over my hips as I walk. I tug it back down and it feels really tight. Too tight. I think back to orientation when Meagan warned us about gaining weight on crappy cafeteria food, and I can't believe I succumbed to such a cliché. Flood, fire drills, and the freshman fifteen all in one weekend! I sigh again as I change into my pink sundress, which isn't really semiformal, but it's the only other dress I packed, and at least it's not form-fitting.

A few minutes later I'm on the buffet line in the student union ballroom when Calvin practically corners me in front of the cheese dip. Tonight he's clean shaven, and he doesn't look so bad in his black pin-striped suit. But he's wearing suspenders, which I always thought were dorky.

"Hey, Cruella. I didn't know you did Science Quiz."

Apparently, he's been doing some Googling of his own.

"Are you stalking me?"

"No. I'm in charge of recruiting, so I had to do some student body research."

"Recruiting for what?" I ask absently as I scope out the room trying to spot Caitlin.

"Some friends and I play team trivia every Thursday night. It'd be great if you could join us one time. We need someone for the science questions."

"I don't know, I'm so busy with schoo—" I jump when I feel my cell vibrating in my purse.

"You okay?"

"Yeah, I just need to take this call," I mutter as I race to the ladies' room, still holding my food plate.

"Wes?" I gasp as I bolt into an empty stall.

"Hey, Dom. How are you doing?" His voice is upbeat, like he just finished a run and is on the endorphin high. If we were together, he'd probably want to have sex right now.

"How am I doing? How are *you* doing? I was so worried about you! I was thinking about calling your parents!"

"Babe, calm down, I'm fine. . . . Are those toilets flushing? You're not in another Porta Potti, are you?" He laughs.

I take a deep breath, realizing I'm literally panting. "No. I'm in the bathroom at a stupid dance. Why didn't you get back to me earlier?"

"I told you I had midterms."

So? When you were on another continent during spring break you still managed to e-mail me every day!

"Right . . . midterms. Sorry, Wes, I didn't think about that."

"I pulled two all-nighters this week, and after the last test yesterday I just crashed. Sounds like you've had a rough time of it too, huh?"

"Tell me about it." I wipe my forehead with some toilet paper. "I got killed on my bio midterm, and my prof was a complete ass to me, so needless to say I'm not feeling my most gung ho about premed. Staying at Chapin's has been fine, but I can't stand not having my own space."

"Well, while you're being exiled, I was sexiled! When I came back to my room after my test yesterday, I opened the door, and there was Gerard, getting head from this chick he's in a play with!"

"Ugh! That's disgusting! Did you ream him out?"

"Nah, the whole thing was pretty funny. I just asked

him to let me know in advance when he'll need the room to 'rehearse' from now on."

I flash back to my failed blow job at the end of the summer, and I start to feel dizzy. I line the toilet seat and sit down, waiting for Wes to invite me to New York. Instead, he starts talking about his training for the marathon.

"Sorry to interrupt, Wes, but JetBlue has a red-eye leaving for JFK in four hours. That way we can have tomorrow together, and I'd come back Monday night. Sound good?" I say all in one breath.

"You know I'd love that, but I have pool duty all Sunday."

"Oh," I say, surprised, thinking that sounds awfully like something he could get out of if he really wanted to. I mean, I'm the one flying hundreds of miles. "There's no one you could switch with?"

"Normally I could, but not with this short notice and on a holiday weekend. Sorry, Dom, I know you need to get away."

"Yeah, well." I don't bother hiding my disappointment.

"Dom, I want to talk more, but I'm supposed to meet up with some people to see a movie, so I better get going."

"Oh, okay, have fun. Who are you going to meet?"

"Jim, Schroeder, Betsy, Kim, Jess, her roommate."

"Wow . . . It's great you've made so many new friends. I know you were worried about having a hard time meeting people."

"Yeah, everyone's great."

"That's awesome. I look forward to meeting them all one day. The people here are great too."

"I'm glad. So I'll call you tomorrow, Dom."

"Sure, okay. I love you, Wes."

"You too. Bye."

I obviously didn't look at the academic calendar very carefully because tonight Chapin informs me Tulane does not observe Columbus Day. I can't afford another bio absence, so as it turns out, not going to New York was the luckiest thing that happened to me all weekend.

30

I fly back to Fort Myers the day before Thanksgiving, which also happens to be Grandma's seventy-fifth birthday. We celebrate by taking her out to high tea. The restaurant Mom chooses this year is in the fancy hotel where Wes and I spent prom night, so it conjures up some nice memories and is a welcome change after Tulane's cafeteria.

Yesterday at the all-dorm meeting Calvin warned us that going home for the first time during college can be disorienting, even depressing. I wouldn't go that far, but it's true everything feels a little different, more provincial somehow. Dad looks shorter, Mom more wrinkled, my room drabber.

Even Fort Myers itself seems gray and dingy. But eating to-gether with Grandma is like old times.

"Dominique, sit up straight!"

"Yes, Grandma."

"Dominique, couldn't you have styled your hair today?" She turns to Mom. "Don't you ever take her to a beauty salon?"

Mom answers calmly, "Dommie landed only two hours ago."

Dad chimes in, "Dom has beautiful hair."

"Styled hair is the ultimate ornament for a lady," Grandma proclaims, lightly patting her red-dyed coiffure. Then she lowers her gaze at me. "And disheveled hair is the surest sign of an unkempt mind."

I roll my eyes as I pop a cucumber sandwich.

"At least your blessings are looking nice and full," she adds, reaching out to pat my left breast.

I jerk away as Dad sputters tea back into his cup. "Grandma, please!" I whisper sharply. Mom's giggling be-hind her napkin.

Fortunately, my phone rings a second later, and I excuse myself even though Grandma gives me her you're-being-terribly-rude look, as if feeling me up during high tea is good table manners. I scurry around booths and service carts to the privacy of the lobby.

"Hi, Wes! Oh my God. We're in driving distance again."

"Heya, Dominique. Howya doin'?" Wes forces a New York accent.

I laugh. "You'll never guess where I am right now. The Sanibel Regal Resort!"

"Where?"

"Um . . . where we spent prom night?"

"Oh, right. Why are you there?"

"It's Grandma's seventy-fifth, so we're taking her out."
Then I whisper, "It's so weird being where we . . . you
know . . . and with my parents!"

"Heh, I bet."

"Anyway, when can I see you?"

"Well, I just landed, and I was going to hang out with
Art for a little and watch some of the *Family Guy* marathon.
Uh, how 'bout I head over to your place around, say, six?"

"Yeah, six is cool. I'll use the extra time in between to
shower and unpack and help Mom in the kitchen and
stuff." Then I whisper, "Um, we'll be able to use the condo,
right?"

"Yeah. My grandparents will be staying in the City until
Christmas. Oh, I see my mom at baggage claim. I better go."

"Say hi to her for me. And, Wes, I'm so looking forward
to being together tonight."

"Can't wait either. Bye."

At 6:18, Wes pulls up in his Explorer. He's wearing a
holey T-shirt, his jeans are ripped, his hair is longer—
almost chin length—and he's completely unshaven. He
smells of the cologne I gave him the night before we left for
college, though, which makes up for his being late.

"Mom freaked when she saw me," he says as I climb in
the passenger seat. "She's dragging me to the barber Friday
morning."

I reach over and French him, which feels funky with his
beard brushing against my cheek. Then I sit back and watch

him as he navigates the holiday weekend traffic on our way to the Captiva condo. To my delight we kiss at every red light, and he keeps his hand on my thigh as he drives. When we're almost there I put my hand in his lap and lightly trace the inseam of his jeans, which makes him hard. We're both so wound up with desire we're not talking much, but we're all over each other as soon as we get in the condo.

Right before he thinks we're about to have sex and asks for a condom, I say, "Actually, I have a Thanksgiving present for you that's way overdue."

"What do you mean?"

I take a package of extra-thin strawberry-flavored condoms out of my purse. "Use one of these this time. I just bought them."

"Why—Oh. Okay."

I huddle over him as he rolls it on, and then without giving myself time to think about it, I drop my head and start licking and kissing the length of his penis. Wes sighs as he crosses his arms behind his head and relaxes his body.

I stop for a second and ask, "Is this okay so far?"

He laughs. "Yeah, I think you can say that."

It occurs to me that hunching over his crotch might not be the prettiest sight, so I pull the blanket over my head.

"Dom." He pulls the covers off. "I want to watch."

Self-consciousness wells up inside of me, and I'm afraid I won't be able to go through with this after all. Somehow it feels more up close and physical than actual sex, and I don't want Wes watching the slobbery mess of it all. But I just have to succeed this time, or else I'll keep agonizing about it.

I close my eyes and take the head into my mouth. I'm afraid I'm going to bite him accidentally, so I keep my lips tightly pursed over my teeth. I get only half of his penis inside before I feel like I'm going to gag. So I continue to suck just the top half of it and bob my head up and down slightly. The more I do it, the more I'm able to fit in my mouth. Unfortunately, the condom does not taste like any strawberry made by nature—imagine sucking on a rubber band dipped in Kool-Aid. I don't know why they call it a *blow* job either, because I'm not really blowing anything, but it *is* a job. My neck and shoulders are sore from bending over, and I barely have sensation left in my jaw by the time he comes.

"Dom . . . I really enjoyed that," he says a few seconds later.

"Well, in that case, I plan to do it often," I say cheerily as I peel off the condom.

Wes sits up. "Now your turn."

"You sure?"

"Hell yeah, I've been wanting to for months, but you said you wouldn't let me until you did it to me first. So now you did."

"I did, didn't I?" I smile.

Unfortunately, it takes a while before we find a comfortable position. First he kneels over me, but this doesn't work because my privates do not project up and out like his. Then I try sitting in one of the steel dinette chairs as he kneels on the floor in front of me, but before he touches me I tell him I can't relax this way—the seat's too hard and cold. Finally I get back on the bed and let my legs hang off the edge. Wes kneels at the foot of the bed and I rest my thighs on his shoulders. This feels right.

Before he starts, he tells me, "Just so you know, I've never gone down on a Tulanian before."

I grab a pillow and whack him over the head.

"You've never gone down on *anyone* before, ever."

"I know, I know." He grins.

Then I remember. "Wait. In my purse, you'll find some dental dams I bought. They're strawberry flavored too. Your favorite."

"C'mon, Dom." Wes sits back on the floor. "We don't need that stuff. I want to taste you, not latex."

"Please, though? It'd make me feel better knowing we're being completely safe."

"You know neither of us has been with anyone else. And in truth, it'd probably 'feel better' without the stupid dams, but you're the boss."

He seems really pissed, so as he rummages through my purse, I say, "Actually, just forget about the dams."

"You sure?"

"Yeah . . . well, you don't have any cold sores or any-thing now, do you?"

"You sure know how to keep a guy turned on, Dr. Dom."

I sit up, wanting to slap myself. "You're right, I'm sorry. I . . . I don't know why I have to be like that. I really didn't mean to wreck the mood."

"Calm down, will you? I was just teasing you. Lie back down and keep quiet. I have work to do," he says sternly as he rips open the dam's packaging.

Amy says oral sex is the absolute best thing a guy can do

to a girl. And she's right—there's none of the pain of pene-
tration. Sex with Wes didn't stop hurting until the eleventh
time we did it, back in July. Even after that it was often uncomfortable, especially in the beginning. But tonight, for
the first time ever I sense a nice, light, pulsing sensation
down there that makes me arch my back, and I can feel my
face get flushed. I wrap my legs around his head and try to
move with him, but suddenly I lose the feeling and don't re-
gain it.

Maybe Wes is right about the dam dulling the pleasure.
Or maybe Amy's right that I'm too self-conscious. But
maybe it's not that simple. What if I'm frigid? Or what if all
my nerve endings down there just don't work? I was always
scared I damaged myself that time in seventh-grade gym
class when I was walking across the balance beam and
tripped, falling straight down onto it with my legs at either
side. Maybe I'll never come, ever.

I can tell Wes is starting to get tired, so I decide to fake
it. I feel bad, but supposedly women do it all the time, and I
want Wes to feel like he's doing well. I also don't want him
to think I'm some asexual freak. I tousle his hair with my
hands and wrap my legs around him tighter as I mimic the
moans I heard Caitlin make that weekend I stayed with her
and Chapin. Finally I yell, "Yes, Wes . . . YEEEES!"

A couple seconds later his face pops up between my
legs. I've never seen him so pleased with himself before.

"Not bad for my first try, eh, Dom? I knew I had it in me."

"Mmm," I sigh, lounging on the bed. "That was
wonderful."

Wes lies down next to me and holds me, but after just a

few seconds he says, "Paul called before and said a bunch of trackies are meeting at Bellini's around nine. Why don't we meet them there?"

"Oh . . . Well, I was sorta hoping we could spend this evening alone."

"I know, but it'll be fun to see everyone again. Maybe Braff will be there."

"No, she won't. She's spending Thanksgiving with Joel and his family in Wichita."

"If you're not up for it, I can drop you home first."

"What? No, Wes, I'm game. Really."

"Cool. But before we do"—he traces the outlines of my lips—"can you, uh . . . again?"

This time I skip the condom, even though I yelled at Amy God knows how many times back in high school for routinely having unprotected oral sex with her random hookups. But Wes isn't random. And right now all I care about is how good I can make him feel, how close we are right now. I'm able to swallow most of his semen as it shoots into my mouth, and I'm surprised at the lack of taste given how much stuff is in it—glucose, fructose, vitamin C, vitamin B12, sulphur, zinc, potassium, magnesium, calcium, copper. It's like a perverted multivitamin.

Dinner at Bellini's turns into dessert at The Bubble Room, which turns into driving to Paul's beach house for drinks, which turns into last man standing. I had no idea Wes had become so much more outgoing. We're in a big group, at least fifteen people, and for the first time he's carrying the conversation and smiling confidently.

At two a.m. on the ride home from Paul's, Wes says,

"You were awfully quiet, Dom. Were you bored out of your mind?"

"No, no, I was just tired from the plane. I had a good time, really . . . anyway, let's make plans. Tomorrow I'll be busy all day with my family for Thanksgiving. But how 'bout we spend Friday and Saturday at Captiva?"

"Eh, the problem is I waited too long to book plane tickets, so the only flight I was able to get back to the City is Saturday morning, not Sunday."

"Oh . . . that really sucks, Wes."

"You're telling me, but I'm free Friday after the barber."

"Um, okay, yeah, I'll take what I can get."

"Cool. I'll give you a call Friday, say, around oneish?"

"Sure."

Before getting out of the car in front of my building, I lean over and kiss him. "Happy Thanksgiving, Wes. I have a lot to be thankful for."

"Me too, Dom." Wes winks at me.

Five minutes later I'm at my computer.

Dear Wes,

First let me say that I completely expected that college would change things a little. And I feel bad complaining, because I did have a good time with you just now and so many things did go right between us. But the fact you were willing to sacrifice part of the night to see old track friends was strange (especially now that you're leaving town early). And it's not like you spent all that much time with them outside of meets last year. I appreciate your trying to include me in the conversation tonight, but I never got to know these people well and I don't get all their little in-jokes, so understandably I couldn't think of anything to contribute. I'm sorry if my reticence bothered you, but c'mon, you used to be reticent too. Anyway, I guess I felt we were a little off tonight, and I wanted you to know so we can work on fixing it, which I know we will. I'm looking forward to having time just for us on Friday.

I love you always and forever, Dominique

I'm about to press SEND when I realize I'm being unreasonable. All Wes was trying to do was maintain his old friendships. And so what if being at NYU is making Wes less reserved? I should be applauding that, not condemning it. I delete the e-mail and go to bed.

31

Friday, the day after Thanksgiving, Wes doesn't call me at one like he promised he would. I pick up the phone to call him but stop myself. I don't want to appear possessive or overanxious. I'm really angry, though. Maybe I should have sent that e-mail after all.

On top of everything, I develop a monster headache waiting for the phone to ring. As I'm searching my parents' bathroom drawers for Tylenol, I come across Mom's diaphragm. The mental image of my parents doing it when I've been waiting all day to do it with Wes is probably the biggest mood-spoiler imaginable, and it takes three tablets before my skull stops feeling like it's being crushed.

When I finally do hear from Mr. Elusive, four hours after the promised time, he sounds completely depressed.

"Wes, are you sure you're up for hanging out tonight?"

"Yeah."

"Are you just in a prolonged food coma or something?" I ask, trying to make him laugh.

Instead, he takes a deep breath. "I'll be over soon."

When I get in Wes's Explorer, he looks as bad as he sounded. I ask him if he's okay, and he says he's just tired.

"Look, Wes." I take out a Tupperware container from my bag. "Chocolate-dipped strawberries!"

"Thanks, Dom." But he doesn't ask to eat one. He doesn't say anything else on the drive to Captiva either. I think back to when we went parking, the night the cop caught us. He was really despondent when he picked me up then too, but it was only because he was lovesick. Maybe this is the same thing?

When we get to the condo, Wes curls up on the bed and stares into space. I tentatively start massaging his scalp and neck, and when he leans into me I move to his shoulders and back, and finally his feet. A few minutes later I work my hands to his crotch, but he's still silent and soft. I lie down behind him, wrapping my right leg over his and wedging my left arm between his neck and the bed so that I can hold him tightly with both arms. I have absolutely no idea what's going on or what to do. Maybe it's me.

"I like your haircut," I whisper, running my fingers through it. "You look more like the old you."

He doesn't answer.

"You know what was really cool? Yesterday morning, I

woke up and my lips were swollen from kissing you. I really miss that feeling at college."

He still doesn't answer.

"Oh, I forgot to tell you. Right before I left I found out I got an A-minus on my last biology test! I'm so relieved. I may be able to pull up my grades after all."

Still nothing.

"You know, if I did or said something wrong, if I upset you in any way, I hope you'd tell me. Please tell me what I can do," I say desperately.

Wes releases himself from my grasp and buries his head in the pillow. It's the first time I've ever seen him cry. His shoulders shake as muffled sobs fill the room.

"Please, Wes, I feel so helpless right now. What's wrong?"

"Jeh . . . sih . . . ca."

Oh God. You're in love with her, aren't you? You've been cheating on me. I always suspected it.

My voice quavers as I speak. "Jessica? Isn't she with her family in Texas now?"

He turns around to face me. "Not her."

"Well, who—Oh." The dog! "Oh no! . . . Is she okay?"

He doesn't answer.

"Is she . . . ?"

He nods and cries even louder, his head now on my shoulder. I turn my face away to hide my look of relief that his sadness has nothing to do with me.

"Oh, I'm so, so sorry. I know she hasn't been doing so well for a while, but I had no idea she was that ill."

"She wasn't. . . . She seemed fine yesterday . . . but she

started having problems breathing this morning . . . while I was at the barber. . . . My dad rushed her to the vet. . . . She had extensive . . . pulmonary . . . meta—, meta—"

"Metastasis?"

He nods.

"That's awful! Did she, um, go naturally or was she put to, you know?"

"To sleep. The vet said she was suffering."

"Poor Jessica. And this all happened today?"

He nods. "This afternoon. I wasn't with her when she died. I should've been. Some Thanksgiving vacation."

I think back to Calvin's warning about the first trip home being strange. That's turning out to be the understatement of the year.

As Wes continues to whimper, I try to make him feel better by reminding him that Jessica lived to an old age, and that her longevity is proof that she had an easy, wonderful life.

"Honestly, Wes, you were the best owner any pet could ever ask for."

Wes sits up and for the first time in our relationship looks at me hatefully.

"Owner? She was *family*."

"Of course," I say quickly, startled at his anger. "Of course I mean family. All I meant was she had the best life a dog could desire, and you should take comfort in that."

His brow furrows like he's thinking about this, and then he slowly sinks back down into the pillow.

I hold him for the next three hours as he alternates between sleep and crying. When he wakes up to the grandfather clock striking ten, he turns over and hugs me.

"Hey. I'm sorry to be a downer, I'm just really, really sad."

"It's totally fine. You're experiencing a massive loss. I just wish there were something I could do or say."

"Thanks for being here. That's enough."

We hold hands while we take a short walk along the beach. I wish he would lift his gaze from the ground to take in the beautiful starlit sky and water, but it's understandable he can't appreciate any of that right now. I tell myself I'm a really horrible person for being disappointed. My boyfriend's dealing with the most traumatic thing that has ever happened to him; meanwhile, I'm just annoyed the dog died during the only time Wes and I have had together in three months. I'm still glad to be with him, but we haven't exactly created any new good memories.

At midnight we're in front of my apartment. Wes's flight is in eight hours.

"I hate this part," I say when I walk around to the Explorer's driver's side window. "Here, take these strawberries for the plane."

"Thanks. Again, I'm sorry, Dom."

"No, no, *I'm* sorry about Jessica. I'm just happy I got to see you. Tell your family I said hi, okay?"

"Sure. Tell your fam I said hey."

"I will. I still can't believe you have to leave tomorrow, with everything you're going through."

"I think it will actually be good to go back to school," Wes says pensively, staring straight ahead. "It'll help get my mind off it."

"Yeah. I'm going to miss you a lot, though. I'm just looking forward to winter break. That's four whole weeks together."

He nods. "That'll be nice."

I lean over to kiss him. He restarts the engine. I just can't hold it in.

"I love you," I bleat as he puts the car into drive.

Please say it. It was bad enough I had to first.

As he rolls up the window, he mouths, "I love you."

Tears stream down my cheeks as he drives away. We didn't make love once this vacation.

32

The following Saturday at seven a.m., I'm speed-walking around Tulane's outdoor track. I'm thinking I'm the only one who could possibly be out this early when I hear, "Good morning, Cruella."

I stop short as Calvin emerges from behind the bleachers. I've managed to avoid him since the freshman semiformal, but he always winks at me whenever we pass each other on campus. Today his sweat-drenched curls are smoothed back from his forehead, revealing a prominent brow line. He has this way of looking straight into my eyes, which makes me uneasy.

I ask, "Isn't it a little early for you to be out and about, what with all the partying you do?"

"I never said I party all the time. I can be serious too. C'mon, it's the weekend, it's beautiful out—let's have a normal conversation."

"What are you even doing here?"

"I work out every morning, and when I saw you walk past the weight room I followed you. Also, I'm worried about you, and I'm sort of responsible for your experience here, as an RA."

"You're not *my* RA," I say as I resume my speed-walking. He keeps up with me. "And aren't you abusing your authority, preying on freshman girls?"

"I'm not preying, I'm concerned. You've been moping around the dorm lately. Why so depressed?"

"You're reading way too much into everything. I'm just preoccupied. Premed's tough, as you discovered the hard way."

"Well, you got me there. . . . So, do you walk here often?" he asks while flicking a mosquito from his forearm.

"Well, I'm thinking of trying out for track, so I started training a few days ago. My best friend runs distance at Amherst, and my *boyfriend* at NYU is a state champion sprinter, so I'd love to be able to keep up with them."

"Ah, I see. . . . Did he give you that mood ring?"

"Yeah. How'd you know?"

"You never stop touching it. It looks like something I once got in a box of Cracker Jack."

"Yeah, well, it means something to me. He *won* it. And I touch it because I miss him."

"As someone older and wiser, let me give you some advice. You two should break up now and agree to stay friends. That way you can keep in touch with none of the pressure, and then there will be a chance you can get together in the long run."

I roll my eyes. "Thanks, Mom."

"I see it every year. A bunch of freshmen come in gabbing nonstop about their significant others. 'My SO this, my SO that.' By the time they're sophomores, they're calling them SOBs. If you cool things down with this guy now, you could go out on a date with me and see what you've been missing."

"Calvin, I'm no more interested in dating you than I would be in dating a horse."

"Even though I'm hung like one?"

I can't help but laugh. Two points for Calvin with the comeback.

"Listen." I stop walking and look at him. "I'm very flattered, but I have absolutely zero desire to date you. If you're cool with that, then I'd be happy to get to know you as a friend. Otherwise, just forget it."

He stares back at me for what seems like a full minute. I shift from foot to foot awkwardly, squinting as the bright morning sun glints off the aluminum bleachers surrounding the track.

Finally he says, "Just so you know, next semester my hall is getting a replacement RA 'cause I'll be studying international business in Paris. So even if we started going out, we'd have to stop when I leave, or else I'd be a hypocrite about the distance thing."

"There, you see? It's all working out for the best." He's obviously missed the point about my already having a boyfriend, but at least it sounds like he's given up on the dating idea. "Hey, Calvin, I'm done warming up, so I'm gonna start running for real now."

"Okay, okay. I do want to be friends, and I'm sorry if I came off as a jerk before. Friends?"

Calvin reaches out his hand, and we shake on it before I take off.

I love these first few seconds of breaking into a run, when you feel the potential for speed coursing through you. That the air has finally cleared between Calvin and me is a huge weight off my shoulders, and my legs must be feeling it too because I'm running my fastest ever. Wes always says he thinks of himself as a jet taking off when he begins a race, and by the time I'm halfway around the track it really does feel like I'm flying . . . until I'm falling.

"Oh shit, shit!" I yell as I land hard on my knees.

Calvin bolts over to me. "What hurts?"

I point to my left leg. It's throbbing so badly I'm scared to look at it. "Is the bone sticking out?"

"Um, no, it looks perfectly fine."

"It hurts so fucking much!" I wail as I lie down on the asphalt to take pressure off my legs.

"Just calm down and take deep breaths," he says in the same authoritative voice he uses in dorm meetings. "Student Health is not that far away. I'll carry you there, they'll assess the damage, and if it's bad, they'll transport you to the ER. Okay?"

"Whatever. I just need help *now*!"

He scoops his left arm under my thighs and extends his right arm around my back. I'm okay with this until I feel his right thumb land on the bottom of my right boob.

"No, don't! Stop!" I yell as if I've been bitten by a rattlesnake.

"What's wrong?"

I disentangle myself from him and balance on my good leg. "Um, what if you drop me? Just call them and have them bring a stretcher or something."

"Okay, okay, have it your way, Cruella." He sighs as he takes out his cell.

An hour later I'm sitting on the doctor's table at Student Health with my left knee wrapped tightly in an Ace bandage. I never knew a first-degree sprain could hurt so much, but it feels much better now that it's bound. The doctor tells me to practice RICE—rest, ice, compression, elevation—and promises I can stop wearing the bandage in about two weeks. However, she advises me to forget about track until sophomore year because my knee may still be too weak for a couple of months.

When she shows me the X-ray, I can identify all the bones and name the ligaments that cover them. She says she's impressed and that I'd make a good doctor. For the first time this semester I feel genuinely eager to do my biology homework.

When I limp my way out of Student Health, I see Calvin waiting at the corner with a campus security golf cart.

"My Ferrari's in the shop. Will this do?"

I crack a smile. "How did you swing this?"

"One of the many perks of knowing the right people

at Res-Life. Your chariot awaits, milady," he says with a slight bow.

"Well, as long as I don't have to tip the driver." I cautiously hobble to the cart and sit beside him.

When he leaves me at our dorm, he says, "I'll check up on you later, and call me if you need me."

"Thank you, Calvin. I appreciate . . . your assistance."

Tonight after Wes and I talk on the phone, he e-mails me a "get well soon" virtual bouquet of daisies. I e-mail back that I'm the luckiest girlfriend in the world.

33

Throughout exam week, if I'm not taking a test or studying at the library, I'm in front of my laptop elevating my leg and shopping online for holiday gifts. I dip into my summer earnings to buy a new book about Matisse for Amy, a CD of viola sonatas for Caitlin, and another year's subscription to *Fishing World* for my parents. For Grandma I decide on a white lace tablecloth because she got so happy reminiscing about her white lace prom dress when I showed her my prom dress, and I thought she could use it for our Sunday brunches.

I give my Tulane friends little sacks of chocolate chip

cookies I bake from scratch in the dorm kitchen. When I go to Calvin's room and hand him one with a note thanking him again for his help at the track, he responds way too enthusiastically with a tight hug.

"What's your IM, Cruella? I want to stay in touch while I'm overseas."

"DominiqueBaylor," I reveal, knowing I can always block him if he gets annoying.

"Don't get married to that guy while I'm away, now."

"I'll e-mail you pics of the wedding," I kid. "Anyway, I gotta go now. Enjoy the cookies."

"Thanks. I bet I'll love them."

I *know* Wes is going to love his Christmas gift—an eight-by-ten glossy photograph that Amy took of us with Jessica the dog at Captiva Beach last summer. Wes has been taking her death really hard and sounds so gloomy on the phone, so I want to do something to help keep her memory alive. In the photo Wes is smiling at the camera and has his arms wrapped around me. Jessica's at our feet, snuggling up to Wes's ankles, and the two palm trees in the background are sort of intertwined. I shell out a hundred dollars for the frame, which is a gorgeous blue glass that matches Wes's eyes perfectly. I get the bottom engraved with the message "In loving memory of Jessica."

Since it'll be his nineteenth birthday just a few days before Christmas, I also buy Wes a track singlet in violet and white, NYU's colors. I ask Caitlin, who's as good with a needle as she is with her bow, to embroider the inside back with the message "For Wes, who makes my heart race. Love always, Dom." It's corny, but true.

The night I get back to Fort Myers, my parents take Amy and me out to dinner in Sanibel to celebrate our successful first semester of college. It's so comforting that the vibe between Amy and me hasn't changed at all since the summer. She looks exactly the same too, except she's wearing a heart-shaped gold locket Joel gave her for the holidays. We're giggling nonstop on the car ride to the restaurant, recounting to my parents all sorts of college horror stories, which mostly involve drunk freshmen peeing off dorm terraces and streaking the quad. I wish Wes could be with us, but he has four more days at NYU.

After we're seated at the restaurant, I announce to everyone I've already received three of my four final grades, and in the unlikely event I failed my last exam, my GPA will still be high enough to keep my scholarship.

"That's fantastic, Dom!" Amy exclaims.

"We're so proud of you, honey," Mom says. "And you had a rough semester too, with your room and your injury." Then Mom opens the menu and mentions how good the veggie stir-fry and steamed tofu dishes look.

I chuckle, "Bland city. You know I always order the nachos and mozzarella sticks here."

She looks down at her menu. "I know, Dommie. I just thought you might want to try something on the healthier side after all that junk food they feed you at school."

"Not a bad idea," I concede. A few seconds later the double meaning hits me. "Wait. Are you saying I'm fat, Mom?"

"No. Did I say that?"

"Basically," I huff.

Amy obviously senses the tension in the air because she excuses herself to go to the bathroom. So I use the opportunity to keep picking a fight. "Trust me, Mom, I've noticed my clothes getting tighter, and I'm dealing with it. But just for your information, my body mass index is still well within what's considered normal. It's also perfectly natural for my metabolism to start slowing down at my age. And by the way, the last thing I need on my first day back is a lecture about a few extra pounds."

"Dommie, calm down, you look beautiful—you always do," Mom persists. "But you're at your best when you're a few pounds lighter."

I sigh exasperatedly. "Dad, are you listening to this?"

He emerges from behind his menu. "I agree with your mom. Guys can be a little overweight," he says, pinching his gut with his hand, "but girls can't."

"Oh my God, that is so sexist and wrong! So what? I'm one size bigger than usual and I'm fat?"

"Not fat, honey, nobody said fat. It's just that cafeteria food. If you eat right the next four weeks, you'll feel lean and healthy by the time you go back."

"Mom, I was taking some very hard classes and trying to maintain an academic scholarship, so it's not like I had any time to exercise. And when I tried to, I injured my knee. You know what, guys?" I throw down my napkin. "Let's just forget this whole meal. I lost my appetite anyway."

"Dom, you're blowing this way out of proportion," Dad reprimands. "We're staying put, and let's have a nice dinner, for Christ's sake."

When Amy comes back, I try to behave myself, but I

know I'm sulking. I was feeling so grown-up today too—a college girl just three days away from turning eighteen—but in the space of ten seconds it's like I'm eight again, Right now I miss the freedom of college almost as much as I miss my boyfriend. When we get home after dropping Amy off, I head straight for my room to sulk some more.

Mom calls out after me, "Make sure to phone Grandma. She said she hasn't heard from you in a while."

I don't care. I know she'll just say something critical, like reminding me to stand up straight. The last thing I need is to feel more self-conscious about my fat self. Especially since Wes will be seeing me naked in ninety-six hours.

34

At noon the following day we get a phone call. Dad picks up since he's home for lunch, and a minute later I hear him call in an anxious voice for Mom, who's in the bedroom grading exams. Something tells me this isn't good, so I emerge from behind my desk to stand in the archway of the living room. Mom's now sitting in the love seat, and her face turns ashen as she clutches the receiver.

"When did it happen?" she asks.

My heart starts racing as I look at Dad, who's gazing sympathetically at Mom and holding her hand. Mom takes down some information and hangs up. Slumped in the love seat, she looks up at me, and says, "It's Grandma. She's—"

Dad immediately kneels down and takes Mom in his arms.

I go to her. "I'm so sorry, Mom," I say, putting my hand on her shoulder. I feel lame not knowing how to comfort her when she's comforted me through so many things all these years. My grandpa's death followed an eighteenth-month-long battle with stomach cancer, so when it finally happened we were sort of prepared for it, and I think Mom was somewhat relieved he wasn't suffering anymore. But this is just so unexpected.

All of a sudden Mom dashes to the bathroom, and we can hear her crying over the running water. Dad knocks on the door but she doesn't respond. He and I keep looking at each other, as if we're hoping the other will give some clue as to what we should do. Soon we go back to the living room where he explains to me that Grandma's cleaning lady, who lets herself in twice a week to straighten up her bungalow, found her this morning in bed, not breathing. She called 911 but it was too late to do anything. Since Mom talked to Grandma yesterday evening, the coroner suspects she had her heart attack sometime last night in her sleep.

Mom eventually emerges red-faced but collected. True to her schoolteacher pragmatism, she immediately picks up the phone and starts making arrangements. Then she calls Amy's mom, asking if I can spend the day over there so I don't have to be home alone while she and Dad are out with the funeral director.

I sit on the couch and watch her helplessly. I can't imagine losing my mom, and it's heartbreaking seeing her so sad. I just wish I felt worse about Grandma's death, if only for Mom to see me reacting appropriately, but I don't. Grandma hadn't been the lovable lady I knew in a long time—she was just sort of deformed by her grief, I guess, and I feel like I mourned her passing years ago.

I really want to talk to Wes about it, but he has an English paper due at midnight and a history take-home final due in two days, so I don't want to take up his time when he's so stressed out. That evening when I come home from Amy's, though, I send him an e-mail. I reason if the situation were reversed, I'd want to know immediately no matter how busy I was.

The next day begins with a small memorial service. I'm standing near the grave with my parents, Amy, the four widows Grandma used to play cards with, and a small group of her neighbors. It's unseasonably warm, and it's strange to think about death when you're surrounded by swaying palm trees and blue skies. It should be cold, windy, and gray, like it was for my grandpa's burial seven years ago, just a few feet from where we are right now. Not even the weather's sad for her.

Mom would be horrified if she knew I was spending most of the funeral thinking about how in two days Wes and I will be making love again. Amy says her mom believes that dwelling on sex is a perfectly normal strategy for coping with death, since sex is the ultimate affirmation of life. That makes me feel better about zoning out during the pastor's eulogy, but it also makes me wonder why Wes didn't want to make love the day Jessica died.

That afternoon Mom, Dad, and I go to Grandma's to start going through her things. While they're in the living room deciding what to keep and what to give to charity, I go to the kitchen and take down all the prom photographs she stuck on her fridge. Just looking at them gives me butterflies in anticipation of Wes's homecoming, and I catch myself smiling.

This isn't right. I need to feel sad. I want to feel sad. I walk down the hallway to Grandma's room and stop at her door, scared to look inside. It's hard to believe she died in there. When I peek in, it looks the same as it always did except for the rumpled bed. I can smell a faint trace of her Chanel No. 5.

I walk to her bureau and look through the drawers. In the top one there's a collection of cards and pictures I made for her when I was little. It takes both hands to scoop them up onto the window seat, where I shuffle through them one by one. There's a card made from pink construction paper, decorated in blue and purple swirls. In a child's scrawl it reads "Happy Birthday, Grandma." I find a picture drawn in Magic Marker of the ocean with stick figures of the two of us on the beach. It reads, "I love you, Grandma."

"Dommie, what are you doing?" Mom's standing in the doorway.

"She kept everything." I hold up a picture I drew of the bungalow. "I don't even remember this stuff."

"I'm not surprised. She saved it all because it meant a lot to her. She really loved you."

"I wish I'd spent more time with her now. I took everything she said too personally."

"She didn't make it easy on you, or us for that matter."

"That's no excuse." I leaf through the cards again.

"Her unhappiness was of her own making. We had only

so much power to change that. I'm just grateful you have so many good memories of her with Grandpa."

Then Mom goes to Grandma's jewelry box and takes out the emerald ring she lent me for prom.

"Grandma wanted you to have it." Mom's voice cracks and her eyes mist over as she hands it to me.

"Oh, Mom . . . are you sure?" I look at her. "I mean, don't you want it?"

She shakes her head. "She was planning on giving it to you for your birthday tomorrow."

I slip it on my left ring finger and hold out both my hands. My mood ring looks dark and lifeless compared to the emerald, which sparkles like green fire.

35

It's almost ten by the time we get home from Grandma's house. I didn't bring my cell to the funeral since it seemed disrespectful, but the first thing I do when I retreat to my room is check e-mail and voice mail. Still nothing from Wes, but I'm not even sure he's reading e-mail, what with his take-home final due tomorrow. I console myself with this thought until Instant Messenger's "invitation to chat" window suddenly appears. I don't recognize the screen name, but I have a pretty good hunch. I'm grinning as I accept the hail.

NYUTrackie: Hey Dom.
DominiqueBaylor: Wes?

NYUTrackie: Yep.

DominiqueBaylor: Hey! XOXOXOOXXOOXOXOXOXXOXOOXXOXOX-OOXOXXOX Did you just change your "The100MeterDash" screen name?

NYUTrackie: I changed it a couple weeks ago, since I made the track team.

DominiqueBaylor: Really? Nice to tell your girlfriend. ☺

NYUTrackie: Sorry. Anyway, I haven't been on IM lately because of exams. I'm really sorry about your Grandma. How are you doing?

DominiqueBaylor: I regret I didn't get to see her one more time since coming home for winter break, but I'm also thankful that she lived as long and as full a life as she did, even if the last few years weren't that great.

NYUTrackie: That's a good attitude.

DominiqueBaylor: The strange thing is I was supposed to call her the night she died. My mom told me I should, but I didn't. I wish I had, though. Last time we talked, she was getting on my case about, I don't even remember what, but it was annoying. I wish we'd had a better last conversation and that I'd gotten to give her her Christmas present.

NYUTrackie: I'm sorry.

DominiqueBaylor: Yeah. Can you believe our birthdays are tomorrow? I'll feel kinda bad celebrating, though, when Mom's mourning, especially on a Sunday. We usually spend Sunday mornings at Grandma's.

NYUTrackie: Yeah, that'll be hard.

DominiqueBaylor: Anyway, how are your finals going? When does your flight get in on Monday?

NYUTrackie: Actually, I've been here since last night. I handed in my take-home early, so I was able to cut out.

DominiqueBaylor: Wait, you're in town?!

NYUTrackie: Yeah.

DominiqueBaylor: Well, congrats on being done with finals. But, Wes, am I wrong for thinking it's a little strange you didn't let me know you were coming home earlier than planned?

NYUTrackie: I knew you were going to be busy with funeral stuff, so I didn't want to intrude.

DominiqueBaylor: Calling to let me know your plans isn't intruding, Wes. I really needed you today. You could have come to the funeral.

NYUTrackie: I'm sorry. I thought that might be awkward for your parents.

DominiqueBaylor: I don't know why—they're well aware you're my boyfriend. But hey, that's water under the bridge. You're here! Now that we're both in town, why don't we ring in our birthdays together tonight? We can spend all tomorrow together too. That'd probably be better for my mom, so she can rest.

NYUTrackie: Actually, I'm pretty tired right now. And I'm not sure what my parents have planned for me tomorrow. Arthur's also in town, so I want to make sure to hang out with him. I haven't seen him since Thanksgiving.

NYUTrackie: You there, Dom?

DominiqueBaylor: Yeah, I'm here. Wes, I don't want to sound whiny, but you haven't seen me since Thanksgiving either. And to be honest, I'm still sort of weirded out you didn't let me know you were coming home early.

DominiqueBaylor: Are *you* there?

DominiqueBaylor: Wes?

NYUTrackie: I'm sitting here with no idea what to write.

DominiqueBaylor: Okay, so call me, then. This isn't the kind of conversation we should be having online, anyway.

NYUTrackie: I would, but I'm over my minutes.

DominiqueBaylor: Oh, really? And to whom have you been talking so much that you've exceeded your minutes? Certainly not to me.

NYUTrackie: Please don't be angry. I was going to call you. But I've been confused, and I wanted some time to think.

DominiqueBaylor: Okay. What are you confused about?

NYUTrackie: I wasn't planning on talking about this tonight. I just wanted to check in about your grandma.

DominiqueBaylor: Well, things don't always go the way you plan them, do they? So again, what are you confused about?

DominiqueBaylor: You there?

NYUTrackie: I don't know how to explain it, or why it's happening. But, Dom, I feel different. I never wanted to feel different. It's just happening.

DominiqueBaylor: You feel different about what?

DominiqueBaylor: About what, Wes? Us?

NYUTrackie: yes

DominiqueBaylor: You want to break up? Is that it?

NYUTrackie: I don't "want" to break up. But, I don't know.

DominiqueBaylor: Well, I do know. I know that you are a liar! On the day we got our college acceptances, you specifically told me that you WANTED to stay together with me!

NYUTrackie: Yes, and also on that day, you said that no matter what, we'd always be friends. Can I count on you to keep your word?

DominiqueBaylor: Wes, how can you expect me to revert to friendship when you aren't acting like a friend? Obviously, you've been having these feelings for a while, and you didn't even tell me until now. Strike that—you didn't tell me at all! I had to force it out of you! I can't even trust you to be honest with me!

NYUTrackie: I'm sorry. But it's a painful thing to tell someone.

DominiqueBaylor: Not nearly as painful as being strung along for the last God knows how many weeks! When did you stop caring for me? Certainly not before Thanksgiving. You certainly wouldn't accept a blow job from someone if you were thinking about breaking up with her.

NYUTrackie: I still care for you a lot, Dom. And I was truly happy to see you over Thanksgiving.

DominiqueBaylor: "Happy to see" me? Just happy to see me? Happy to get head, is that it? But not happy enough to have sex.

NYUTrackie: That never went through my mind, I never thought of you just physically. But I started to feel different then too. I didn't want to, so I tried to ignore it. I just didn't want us to mess around this vacation until I had it sorted out. I guess that's why I didn't call you earlier.

DominiqueBaylor: Yeah, but, Wes, isn't it normal to feel that way after being apart for so long? I mean, wasn't that the purpose of winter break? For us to see a lot of each other again and get reacquainted and get as close as we were before? In my opinion, everything you're feeling is normal and fixable.

DominiqueBaylor: Wes???

NYUTrackie: Dom, I really don't think so. You see, it used to be like a craving, wanting to see you again, but now it just doesn't occur to me as much. I don't know exactly when it started happening. Maybe if we had gone to the same school things would have been different.

DominiqueBaylor: YOU FUCKING ENCOURAGED ME TO GO TO A

DIFFERENT SCHOOL!! YOU WERE THE ONE WHO CREATED THIS SITUATION!!!

NYUTrackie: I didn't mean for any of this to happen, Dom. I'm really sorry. But look at it realistically—we're just teenagers.

DominiqueBaylor: "Just teenagers." Well, excuse me for thinking like a mature adult and not an overgrown adolescent.

DominiqueBaylor: There's someone else, isn't there?

NYUTrackie: No. Well, no one in particular.

DominiqueBaylor: Do you have any idea how many dates I turned down these last four months because YOU told me you wanted to stay together?

NYUTrackie: I feel bad about that. I guess I should have handled things differently.

DominiqueBaylor: You know, it's so fitting that in track you're a sprinter and you suck at distance running. You can't go the distance! If I hadn't confronted you like this, would you even have had the guts to break up with me this vacation?

NYUTrackie: I don't know. I guess I'd have to. I really hadn't thought about it lately, Dom, I was so busy with finals and tryouts. I tried to put it out of my mind these last couple of weeks. I just didn't want to think about it.

DominiqueBaylor: You "didn't want to think about it"??? I think about you ALL THE TIME. I was busy as fuck this semester too, and I still thought about you ALL THE TIME.

DominiqueBaylor: I do need to hear it, Wes. Or read it, since you're too much of a cheapskate to call me. Say you don't love me.

DominiqueBaylor: Say you don't love me.

NYUTrackie: I guess I don't anymore in the way I used to, but you still mean a lot to me. I'm sorry if I ruined your birthday.

DominiqueBaylor: You know, that's the most insulting thing I've ever heard! Today is not my birthday. Today is the day we buried my grandma. Tomorrow is my birthday, and it's gonna be a lot better without you around lying to me. You must have totally underestimated me all these months to think I would actually let you ruin my birthday.

NYUTrackie: Dom, *please* don't end it like this. I don't want us to stop being friends.

DominiqueBaylor: You were the one who ended it like this, and you don't know how to be a friend. You weren't even man enough to tell me all this to my face. Have a nice life, Wes. I won't be playing any part in it.

I sign off before he can reply.

PART IV

36

10:59 p.m.

Wait a second. I sit back in my chair. Did what just happened happen?

I jump up and stand in front of my full-length mirror. I don't look any different. But it's like I've never seen myself before, like I've been plucked from real life and dropped in a prison cell that looks like my room. I lower my gaze to my hands, which now feel like alien appendages. I punch them against the wall. Then again, harder. This isn't real.

Stop it! I shake my head. This is nuts. I'm fine. There's no reason why I'm not fine. I'm still me. Still me.

I knock on my parents' door.

"What's wrong, Dommie?" Mom croaks as I come in. Dad switches on the nightstand light.

"Mom, Dad," I say crisply. "I'm really sorry to wake you, but I wanted to let you know we broke up."

Their jaws drop in unison as they look straight at me. After a beat Dad says softly, "Really?"

I flinch. The possibility that maybe it didn't really happen shoots through me like electricity. But I'm not that delusional.

I lean against the cedar door frame. "Are you both happy now?" I snap without meaning to.

"All we want is for *you* to be happy," Dad counters. "And it's his loss, you know."

I roll my eyes and laugh. "Right."

Mom says, "The important thing is now you can go back to Tulane with no strings attached. It'll be a new beginning."

"Yeah, the beginning of being alone," I mutter. When my parents don't respond, I realize how terrible I am for complaining to them, considering we were at a funeral just twelve hours ago. So I take a deep breath and say, "Anyway, that's all I needed to tell you."

Dad asks, "You sure you don't want to talk more about him tonight?"

I look at him like he's crazy. "Dad, I don't want to talk about him *ever again*!"

"Okay," Dad says. "That's fine."

After another silence Mom smiles. "We'll have a nice birthday for you tomorrow."

I nod. "Dad, I want to go fishing in the morning."

"You do?" His eyes gleam.

"Yeah. I want to catch buckets full, and then I want them for dinner."

"Well, there are plenty of fish in the sea," Mom says buoyantly.

I look at her disgustedly. How can she joke at a time like this? I slam their door behind me and don't say good night. I hear Mom get out of bed and Dad say to her, "No. Let her alone for a while."

11:04 p.m.

My knuckles hurt. I rub them on my way to the kitchen, where I search the cabinets for a big black garbage bag. Mom's right. I've got to *cancel and move on.*

Back in my room I stuff the bag with all my framed photographs of us, including the engraved one I was going to give him for Christmas. Why do people even take photographs, anyway? They're just reminders of what once was, of what you'll never get back. It's so masochistic.

Next to go are the vegetarian cookbooks and four issues of *Runner's World,* which I used to toss around my room before he'd come over so he'd be impressed by the common interests I pretended we had. Then I throw out the manila envelope I used to hold ticket stubs of movies we went to together but didn't really watch because we were making out in the back row.

After laying down the bag I stare at my computer screen. Every word he wrote me this past year I used to think was so priceless. Now they're all meaningless, not even worth the RAM they occupy. I click on the "Wes" folder, where I stored all our old e-mails, JPEGs, and transcripts of IM chats, and drag it to the trash. I block his screen name on Instant Messenger, delete all my bookmarked Web sites having to do with him, and cancel his name from my online address book. Then I erase his number and old text messages from my cell phone. I wish I didn't know his number by heart. I wonder how long it will take me to forget it . . . or if I ever will.

I shut down my computer and slide open my closet. I take my prom dress and hang it inside an opaque garment bag. A bunch of Wes's dead skin cells probably still cling to the green silk, and I don't ever want to lay eyes on it or be reminded of that night. Then I bundle together my prom shoes and purse and place them out of sight on the highest shelf, which is where I come across the pressed yellow and red rose corsage. I hold it over the garbage bag and crumple the crusty petals with my fingers until they're nothing but dust.

Next I open my top dresser drawer and pull out the track singlet I was going to give Wes for his birthday. I wrapped it so beautifully. He would have liked it so much. He would have looked so fucking hot in it. I bet he didn't even think to get me a birthday present, or a Christmas present. He wouldn't have wanted to encourage our sham of a relationship with gifts. I shove the singlet in the trash.

I stand up in the middle of my room and scan for any remaining traces of him. My *Princess Bride* DVD on the bookshelf catches my eye, and I throw it in the bag immediately. There's no way I can ever enjoy watching it again, with the hero's name being Westley. A perfectly good movie ruined.

Then I spot the holiday card on my desk, already sealed

and stamped, that I was going to mail to Wes's parents to-morrow. As I drop it into the garbage, it hits me that I didn't just break up with Wes, I broke up with his family! Despite the son they spawned, I really like Mr. and Mrs. Gershwin. I hope they'll miss me too. Or maybe they just won't care.

Last, I deposit the mood ring into the bulging bag. Calvin was right at the track that day—it is a cheap piece of shit.

I forcibly yank on the drawstrings and tie them in a triple knot. I want to drop-kick the whole thing into the Dumpster downstairs, and I actually open my window and peer down to the ground, calculating where it would land.

Damn it. I can't get rid of this stuff. Not yet.

I hoist up the bag and shove it in my bathroom linen closet behind a pile of towels.

11:21 p.m.

On the middle shelf of the linen closet I see my maxi pads, which remind me of the condoms and lube tucked away in the storage box underneath my bed. As I reopen the trash bag and throw away these graphic reminders, I suddenly feel hollow, empty, dried up. Wes will never be inside of me again, ever, even though I'll have to live with the memory of what I'm missing forever. How is it that mankind can engineer condoms to prevent pregnancy and STDs and not be able to invent some sort of emotional safeguard? Is it even possible to *abstain* from falling in love?

I go back to my desk, flip open my cell, and stare at the keypad. I want to hear his voice so badly, to be connected to him, to ask him why and how and what I can do to make it better. But you can't force someone to love you.

I hate being this powerless. I hate no longer having license to kiss him. I hate feeling grief while he's probably just feeling relief.

11:29 p.m.

"Hello? Dom?"

"Hey," I choke out. "I know it's late, sorry."

"It's okay."

"I'm . . . in such utter disbelief right now. . . . It hurts so much. I can't believe this is happening to me."

"I'm really sorry, Dom . . . but it's a normal reaction to someone dying."

"No! This isn't about my grandma!"

"Well, wha—?"

"Amy—" I start crying and curl up on the bed. "Wes just dumped me."

A pause. "Oh shit! Oh, Dom. Dom, I am so sorry."

"Just an hour ago I had a boyfriend . . . and now I don't and probably never will again. And we broke up over IM! IM!!"

"Oh my God! Okay, that's majorly sucky on his part. Ugh! You know, my roommate told me that in Malaysia, a man can legally divorce his wife over a text message."

I sniffle. "Um, if you're trying to make me feel better, it's not working."

"Sorry, I'm sorry. So Gersh just sprang this on you now?"

"Well, I knew he'd been acting sorta distant lately, and he hadn't really said the l-word since before Thanksgiving . . . but I kept justifying his behavior. You know, in mourning for the dog and stressed out from school."

"Well, yeah. Plus, Gersh was never the demonstrative type."

"Exactly, and I assumed that when we saw each other again it'd be fine. But, Amy . . . I think I knew it wouldn't be fine. Deep down. I just didn't want to admit it to myself."

"So what did he say?"

"Just that his feelings changed, but there has to be more to it, right? Maybe I wasn't as smart or interesting as his New York friends. . . . Oh my God, do you think it was my freshman fifteen?" I think back to our Thanksgiving hookup. I must have looked like such a cow while I was going down on him.

"At the risk of sounding like my mom, a few extra pounds do not make or break a healthy relationship."

"Ames, we had all these plans! He was going to come down for Mardi Gras and meet all my friends. What am I going to tell them now? They'll think I'm such a loser! Oh no, I'm going to have to change my status to 'single' on My-Space now. What if I wind up like my parents, desperate enough to answer personal ads?"

"Okay, calm down. Relationships end. People understand that." She hesitates for a second. "I mean, isn't it better to end by a breakup now rather than a divorce later, or death? My dad's still reeling from divorcing Mom, and that was years ago."

"Honestly, I think I'd feel better if Wes were dead."

"You don't really mean that."

"I do. I still love him so much, Ames," I gurgle. "And I feel so worthless because he doesn't love me anymore."

"Listen, do you want to talk to my mom? She hasn't gone to bed yet, and she dissects relationships for a living."

My stomach rumbles.

"Dom?"

"No, I . . . I actually feel sick. I need to go—"

"Dom, you're going to be fine. Dom?"

11:38 p.m.

I race to the bathroom and take a massive shit, expelling so much so quickly my whole abdomen cramps up. I hug both knees into my chest, but that only makes the pain worse, like my intestines are trying to strangle me from the inside out. Then I go some more.

After flushing, I kneel over the tub and cry the hardest I ever have. I have to run the bathwater to drown out the wails—the last thing I want is Mom busting in with Kleenex. Soon the entire bottom half of my face is covered with snot, and the grotesque contortions of my sniveling mouth and cheeks strain my throat muscles and make it hard to swallow.

11:59 p.m.

I feel like I've cried to the point of severe dehydration, and my body is trembling all over, so I slog to my bed and lie down. I clutch my cell phone, hold my breath, and count down the seconds to my birthday—our birthdays. Maybe if I hope hard enough, want it badly enough, he'll call.

At midnight my lungs are screaming for air, but I keep holding it in. Then it rings.

I gasp as I tighten my grip, causing the phone to slip out of my sweaty hands. I fumble it like a hot potato for three rings before regaining my hold.

Amy's name flashes on the display. I hurl the cell across the room. It lands on the exact spot on the carpet where

Wes kissed me for the first time. Then I remember the Dave Matthew's "Crash" MP3 that accompanied our first kiss. Ten seconds later it's erased from my hard drive.

12:02 a.m.

I'm on my terrace gazing down at the parking lot, six stories below. If I jumped headfirst, I'd probably die on impact, and Wes would blame himself . . . or would he? He'd definitely feel bad, but he'd probably also think I was completely unstable, which would just make him more relieved we didn't end up together. He must already think I'm some psycho bitch after the horrible things I said on IM, not that he didn't deserve it.

No, I'd never kill myself . . . but it surprises me how easy it is to think about. I wonder . . . if I just *approach* suicide, not going all the way but far enough to look death in the face, maybe that one terrifying moment will put Wes into perspective and make me grateful just to be alive.

I grasp the handrails with straightened arms and bend my knees so that the railing is supporting my entire body weight. I lean forward a few degrees. Then a few more. When I look down, my elbows start shaking and I get a quick rush of fright prompting me to push away from the bar and jump back on my legs.

I don't feel any better. Just more pathetic.

12:05 a.m.

I return to my bedroom and boot up my computer. I unblock his name on my buddy list to see if he's on. He is. I wait for a couple minutes to see if he hails me. He doesn't. I block him again.

I bet he's chatting now with his NYU friends about how crazy I acted. Or maybe I'm not coming up in conversation at all. Or what if he's telling them about the first time I tried to give him a blow job and didn't get further than that ugly, awkward hunch over his dick? How inane I must have looked. How pitiful he must think I am. That's probably the most lasting image he'll carry of our relationship—me crouching over his dick, not sucking it . . . or me lumbering, mud-covered, to a Porta Potti. Suddenly my esophagus becomes a geyser and I rush to the bathroom again.

12:20 a.m.

My head is still dangling over the toilet, now filled with an acid and enzyme puree of the night's takeout veggie burger dinner. This is the first time I've thrown up in almost a year, since the day I met Wes at the EFM football game, and I forgot how disgusting it feels. I hate my body for being so weak and frail, for mirroring my emotions rather than rising above them. Soon the dry heaving takes over.

12:34 a.m.

My back is sore from my barfing spasms. My throat's raw from all the puke. With my stomach knotted from shitting and my neck strained from crying, I no longer have enough range of motion to extract my limp body from my vomit- and mucus-encrusted black polyester funeral dress. Too worn out to cry anymore, I crawl on all fours from the bathroom to my bed. At some point in the middle of the night I fall into a still sleep and don't dream.

37

At half past nine I wake up with my usual thoughts of Wes. I feel calm and excited for our birthdays until my memory floods back. Yesterday really happened. My lower back is sore. My throat is dry. My right hand is lifeless without the mood ring. But other than that, I feel . . . okay. I'm eighteen. I'm eighteen today.

I stretch my arms up and look out of the window over my headboard. It's beautiful outside. I cling desperately to the hope it brings. I really need to pee, but instead of rushing to the bathroom I dive onto the floor to retrieve my cell phone. It's chipped on the right side and the display is cracked, but it's still working. No calls. I race to my computer and check my e-mail.

My heart literally rattles in my chest when I spot Wes's name couched between two birthday e-cards sent by Tulane friends. There's no subject line, and it's only one kilobyte. *Please, please make this say what I want it to say!* I click open the message.

Subject:
Date: Sunday, December 22, 1:02 a.m.
Dom, I'm really sorry how things turned out. Please don't hate me. W

After rereading it a few times, I click REPLY.

Dear Wes (a.k.a. Fucking Bastard),

Please don't *hate* you??!! I hate that I *love* you. Loving you made me waste a year of my life. Loving you made me be passionate about nothing but you. Loving you made me take risks I never would have otherwise. Loving you made me give it up to you. Loving you made me neglect my parents and Amy. Loving you made me not care that my grandma just died. Loving you made me turn out bitter and hopeless like her. Loving you made me hate myself for being dumped by you. Loving you made me deluded, irrational, inconsiderate, and a liar. And because I love you, you're always going to haunt me.

I'll never be able to have another birthday without wondering how you're celebrating yours. I'll never be able to think another guy is more handsome, talented, intelligent, or worth loving than you, despite all your faults (and there are many). I'll never be able to check my e-mail without praying I'll find a message from you with the subject line *I love you, Dom—please come back to me*. Meanwhile, every corner of this city is laced with memories of us together, and I'll never be able to leave the house without hoping and dreading that I'll run into you. You stole Fort Myers from me, and I lived here first, you fucking thief. You actually may be one of my last thoughts when I die.

It's really no surprise you suck at relationships. As an English major and a trackie, you devote yourself to activities that require no real teamwork. You don't know the first thing about what it takes to play off of each other and achieve a common goal. You were on the bench the whole time, leaving me with all the exhausting work of keeping our relationship going until you just called "game over."

So fuck you. Have a happy fucking birthday.

Dom

P.S. Remember the night before Thanksgiving? I faked it!

Before deleting the e-mail, I print it out and stuff it in the Wes trash bag in my bathroom, I guess in a symbolic attempt to throw away my feelings for him.

Suddenly I wonder if Wes's dumping me is some sort of karmic retribution for my rejecting Calvin so callously. Then I think how a true scientist would never be so superstitious. I immediately grab my Operation board game and also shove it in the trash, not because it reminds me of him, but because it reminds me of how pathetic I am.

Finally, I park on the toilet and let myself pee for the first time this morning, and I can feel myself fall into despair, deeper than ever. I'm still in my black dress, and I smell.

After stripping I trudge to the shower. I try to shave my legs, but my hands shake so much I keep cutting myself. I watch the blood trickle down my shins. Even this reminds me of Wes, of the day he pulled me from the mud. My knees still have scars from that fall. I'm always going to have them.

I increase the temperature of the shower until it's scalding, and I force myself to stand still under the stream. I want to be cleansed, reborn, exorcized, revirginized, something. All I get is overheated.

"Happy birthday to our now legally adult girl!" Dad exclaims when I plod into the dining room.

Mom's bustling around the table, affixing balloons and streamers to the wall. She comes down from the stepladder and walks over to hug me. I raise my arms in stiff reciprocation. I can tell from her puffy eyes she's been crying about Grandma, but she manages a weak smile as she asks, "How does it feel to be eighteen?"

So far, it sucks, I want to scream in her face.

"Whatever. Same as always."

"You all right, Dom?" Dad asks from his place at the head of the table. "Sure you don't want to talk about—"

"Yes, Dad," I grumble through gritted teeth.

"You're still up for fishing, I hope? It'll get your mind off things."

"Yeah, maybe." I take my usual seat and pour myself some ice water even though I have zero thirst.

Mom carries in a colorful assorted fruit platter. As she's serving me she says, "Be sure to sit up straight, honey."

I almost drop the pitcher out of shock. I thought that whole posture business died with Grandma. Instead, it's been passed on. And Mom's not giving me a break, today of all days! I know I should take the high road and fake being happy, but when she asks a minute later what I'm planning to do for the rest of the break, I lose it.

"Well, Mom, I was intending to spend my highly anticipated and well-earned vacation with my boyfriend. But since my winter break has turned into a winter breakup, I guess I'm going to have to come up with a Plan B. Thanks for reminding me that I've just been dumped, Mom. How sensitive of you."

I run back to my room, lock the door, and flop down on the bed. I can't hold it in anymore, and I start sobbing again.

"Dom, it's Dad. Please let me in."

"No," I cry. "Leave me alone."

"Let me in, Dom. I'm not leaving."

"Jesus. Fine!" I scream as I open the door.

He's standing there with a small wooden lockbox. He says softly, "Dom, sit with me a minute. I want to show you something."

"Please, I want to be alone."

"Just look." He closes the door behind him. "This won't take long."

I grab a tissue and reluctantly plop down on the bed next to Dad. He lifts open the top of the lockbox and takes out a photograph.

"Is that you?" I sniffle, pointing to a thin man with brown hair and a wide smile.

"Yeah. I was twenty."

"Who's that?" I point to a blonde who has her arms around Dad's waist.

"Sandra, the girl I was engaged to before your mom. We went to Florida State together."

I immediately stop crying. "You were engaged before Mom?" I study the image more closely. "Yech."

"C'mon, Sandy was attractive."

"Mom is so much prettier." I study the woman, the woman Dad wanted before Mom. "So, why didn't you marry her?"

"I wanted to. We were together for five years, but she broke it off."

"Five years?"

Dad nods. "At the beginning, we were crazy for each other. I never stopped being crazy for her, but she just grew apart from me, I guess."

After a silence I ask, "How long did it take for you to get over her?"

"A while, and—I won't lie, Dom—it felt like taking a bullet."

"Great," I say dejectedly as I start picking at the new scabs on my legs. "Why did I have to love him so much if we're not going to end up together?"

Dad sighs as he shuts the box. "It's one of life's mysteries. What baffled me about Sandy was I wanted to be with her even though I could've made a list of a hundred good reasons why we were wrong together. Anyway, after she left, I realized that even though I couldn't control my feelings, I had complete control over my actions. It hurt, but I chose to get out there again and see other women, and then I met the right woman. Whatever I felt for Sandy eventually went away."

"I just feel so stupid I'm in this situation at all. All the thoughts I'm having—it's like I'm insane."

"You're not, take my word for it. I know from my Sandy days what a roller coaster this is for you."

"Mom doesn't get it, though. She's never been through this."

"That's true, and I feel kind of sorry for her."

I look at him incredulously. "You feel sorry for Mom that she's never been heartbroken?"

"In a way. She's never experienced the big lows that make the big highs so much better." Dad's looking off into space now and pats the lockbox with his hand. Finally he punches my shoulder gently and says, "C'mon. Let's go back to the table, and you should apologize to Mom for yelling. Remember, she just lost her mommy. She's putting on a brave face, but you gotta be extra good to her."

"Yeah, okay."

"And don't tell her about Sandra." He pats the box again. "She doesn't need to know."

"I won't. And Dad?"

"Yes, Dom?"

I hug him. "Thanks."

38

Our fishing trip lasts only twenty minutes because I can't stop regurgitating breakfast over the side of the boat. Then the next two days continue my vicious cycle of sporadic crying, puking, checking e-mail, writing e-mails I don't send, hoping, wallowing, and bitching to Amy about Wes. I guess I'm testing her patience because she's being unusually quiet on the phone, and I have to keep reminding her to give me her opinion.

I muster the self-restraint not to call Amy on Christmas Eve, to give her a break. But she calls me a little after ten while I'm trying to go to sleep. I've already been in bed most of the day except a half hour for breakfast and a half hour for dinner, which my parents wouldn't let me skip.

"Hey, Ames," I choke. "Merry almost-Christmas."

"Dom, I know you're dealing with a lot and I'm so sorry, but I actually really need you right now. Can you come over?"

"Well, what's wrong?" I ask, looking at my alarm clock. "It's late."

"*I'm* late."

After a beat: "How late?"

"Ten days."

"Holy shit, Ames." In a flash I'm sitting up and my heart starts racing.

"I've been late before, but never more than four or five days, so I'm officially freaking out, Dom."

"I thought you were using condoms."

"We do, but those things can break."

"Did you tell Joel?"

"No. I don't want to unless I'm sure." Her voice cracks. "Even then I'm not sure if I'd tell him."

Within minutes I'm on my bike. It feels good to be outside moving again, though I'm amazed my muscles are still operating normally after forty-eight hours on my back. On the way to Amy's I stop at the twenty-four-hour CVS, the same one where I bought condoms, lubricant, and dental dams in the past eight months. Today, I buy a pregnancy test.

I wait on Amy's Papasan chair while she uses the bathroom. Fifteen minutes pass before Amy admits she's too scared to pee. I advise her to run the faucet and visualize a peaceful scene of gushing streams and waterfalls. After another ten minutes she manages to squeeze enough drops into a Dixie cup, into which she dips the test strip. I hold her hand for the next three minutes as we watch for the results to take shape. It's bizarre to see Amy freaked out about something sex related.

"Dom, what if I'm pregnant?" She undoes the clasp on her heart locket necklace and flings it against the shower curtain. "Fucking sperm!"

"Let's not worry unless there's something to worry about."

Soon Amy's holding the negative test strip to her heart and crying, "Oh, thank God! Thank God! Thank God! It's a fucking Christmas miracle!" She grabs my hands and jumps up and down on her bath mat whooping for joy. "I have never wanted to be a nun as much as I do now," she says finally.

"I'll believe that when I see it." I laugh. "Anyway, it's probably training for track that did it. Changes in exercise habits often throw menstrual cycles out of whack. You should see a doctor if you don't get it soon, though."

"Oh, Dom," she pants, fanning herself with her hands. "There's no one at Amherst I could have gone through this with. You're the best!"

We hug, and I get her a cup of cold water from the sink. She downs the whole thing.

"Thanks," she says while refilling the cup. "I feel so much better."

"It's okay. Honestly, as much as this sucked, it was actually kind of nice to have something on my mind other than you-know-who."

"Speaking of which," Amy says as she wipes her eyes and sits on the toilet seat. "Now that I can stop being completely self-absorbed, how did today go? How's your back?"

I sit down too, on the edge of the bathtub. "It's totally sore from all the barfing. Ever since it happened I can't keep anything down."

Amy nods before taking another sip of water. "Remember how Mom said lovesickness is like a crash diet?"

"Yeah, well, I'd rather chip away at my freshman fifteen in a healthy way. Biking here was the first exercise I've gotten since I hurt my knee."

"You should go biking again tomorrow. Being cooped up in your room all day's not going to help you."

"I know, but at least it's a foolproof way not to run into him."

Just then the Braffs' living room clock strikes midnight. I motion for Amy to follow me back into her room, where I open my knapsack and hand her the art book I bought.

"I was going to wrap it and give it to you tomorrow, but after you called I thought I'd bring it over now as a 'congrats on not being p.g.' gift, hoping it was a false alarm. And now that it's officially Christmas—"

"Oh, Dom! Thank you so much! Matisse is Joel's favorite too." As she flips through the pages her expression turns from ecstatic back to somber. "I, um—" She holds the book to her chest and looks at me guiltily. "I made your Christmas gift."

"You painted me something?"

"It was an acrylic portrait . . . of you and, well . . . I assume you'd rather not have it now?"

"Oh, Ames. I—" I cover my face in my hands as the tears

come. "I feel so bad. I really don't think I can look at it right now. I'm so sorry. I'm really touched you did that. He probably would have been too. Shit."

"It's fine, Dom, I'm not offended. It wasn't one of my best." She laughs. "Anyway, after everything happened, I bought you something instead." Amy opens her closet and hands me a wrapped box. "I thought it might help."

I start pulling at the bow, but Amy grabs my arm. "Actually, don't open it until you're home. And make sure you're alone."

"Why?"

"Trust me on this one."

39

At half past midnight I'm on my bed opening Amy's present. The photograph on the packaging shows a man holding some kind of bulbous wand to his neck. I flip the box over—the label reads "personal massager." I guess she really was concerned about my sore back.

I plug the power cord into the outlet behind my nightstand and lie down on my stomach. I take the massager and run it over my shoulders and spine. It doesn't feel that great and the buzzing noise is beyond annoying. I also can't maneuver it without twisting my arms behind my back, which only makes the original pain worse. What a piece of junk.

I switch it off and flip over, wondering how I can tell Amy I'm going to return it. But why was it important to her that I open this when I'm alone?

Then it dawns on me. Like Amy really gives a damn about my sore muscles. God, I'm slow.

But how can she actually expect me to use this now, after everything that's happened? Because of Wes, I feel more miserable, hopeless, and perpetually nauseated than I knew was humanly possible. Grandma's death is looming over my family. My heart rate still hasn't returned to normal since Amy's pregnancy scare. Not to mention the fact that my parents are in the very next room. I've never been less in the mood to attempt to have my first orgasm, with a vibrating piece of plastic, no less.

On the other hand . . . maybe that's the whole point. To do something separate from all of that, for myself and by myself. To take back control of my body in some small way.

But what if I use this and it just doesn't work? If man and machine both fail, maybe there really is something wrong with me. That will only make me feel worse.

I'll never know unless I try.

I leap up and lock my door. Then I throw the empty box into the back of my closet where no one will see it. Next I go to my computer to load a playlist of MP3s to drown out the buzzing sound. Finally I draw the shades over my window so no one in the neighboring apartment building can see in.

I kick off my jeans and toss them on my desk chair. After a quick mental debate, I take off my undies too. I pull up my covers and tuck my gift in underneath. I decide to go for the gold, so I set the massager on high and rest it between my legs.

Holy!

My body scoots away so fast I bang up against the head-board. That was way too intense.

I think I need a little buffer, so I decide to place the mas-sager on the other side of the blanket. I also turn the setting down to the lowest level and take things more gradually this time. I set the massager on my calves first. Then my thighs. Then up over my pubic hair. Meanwhile, I slowly tickle my belly and breasts with my left hand. I can't believe I am doing this! It's like I'm seducing myself, and the thought makes me laugh out loud.

I close my eyes and try to relax. After a few minutes I spread my legs and rest the head of the massager over my genitals. It feels promisingly good. There's certainly some-thing new and different here that I'd felt only hints of be-fore with Wes—heavier tingles, and a deep pulsing. Soon a pleasant weakness spreads down my arms and legs. I defi-nitely don't want to stop.

Almost instinctively, with my right hand I start to move the machine up and down, from the top of my pubic hair line to the sheets. It feels good everywhere, but I start nar-rowing in on one particular spot, right above my vagina. More tingles and pulses. My heartbeat quickens, and I hold my breath. Suddenly it's as if a huge passageway opens up down there and all my body's energy is racing toward it. Then, an eruption. My hips thrash up and down like crazy, and I grunt as if I have just been kneed in the stomach.

I toss the massager aside as the heavenly pleasure con-tinues to wash over my body. I moan again as I feel my lips and cheeks contort. After four or five seconds, the undulat-ing spasms stop, and it's like I'm . . . floating.

After a moment of sheer shock, I begin to cry. Crying for everything—relief that I'm capable of coming; regret that I hadn't done this to myself sooner; sadness I couldn't share it with Wes; and more than anything, gratefulness that, for a few seconds at least, I forgot all about him. Then, out of all my feelings, one rises to the top. Curiosity. Could I do this again? And could it be even better?

My tears subside as I reach for the massager. I conjure up my fantasy of being chased on the beach, except this time Amy's stepbrother subs in for Wes. I sweep the machine up and down again and again, and just when it starts feeling amazing, I take it away, stop for a moment, and start again. I do this for what seems like forever until I finally let myself come.

"Dom, you okay in there?" I hear Dad ask from the other side of my door.

"Yeah," I struggle to say. "I bumped my shin against the stupid desk. Sorry I woke you."

"Well, be careful. And Dom, can you turn down your music? Mom and I are trying to sleep."

"Sure, Dad." I stifle a giggle as I stagger to the speakers.

I unplug Amy's present and hide it in the bottom drawer of my nightstand beneath a couple of bathing suits. Soon the clock strikes one, and I smile, realizing this has been an okay Christmas no matter what happens or how I feel in the morning. It's like I have just discovered a new color, or have finally grown into my skin. I can't blame Amy for being unable to describe an orgasm, because it's so . . . all over the place, like a combination of receiving a foot massage, jumping on a trampoline, getting tickled, rolling downhill, and peeing after holding it in for three hours. Imagine all that concentrated into a few divine seconds. The human body really is incredible.

Despite my newfound power, not one second of winter break passes without my wanting him back. Although I manage to ride my bike every day, my heart stops whenever I see a blue Explorer turn the corner. I'm constantly checking my cell phone to see if he called. And I write him dozens more e-mails—some angry, some apologetic, some just pure begging—which I have the sense never to send. When Mom comes into my room the night before I go back to Tulane and sees my eyes are red from crying again, she loses it.

"That's it, I just can't take it anymore! It's been three weeks and you're still miserable! You're so much better than this, Dommie. If he can't see how wonderful you are, then he's the one with the problem, not you!" She looks at me with doting but frustrated desperation. "I don't want to sound harsh, honey, but *cancel and move on, damn it!*"

I'm not mad at her. She just has no idea. It's actually kind of cool that there's an area of life where I'm actually more experienced than my own mother.

"Mom. Everything you're saying makes sense. Perfect sense. But what happened to me in the last year is something not based on sense."

"What's it based on, then? What's the solution?" Her voice is cracking.

"I'm not sure, but I can't automatically stop loving him."

"I just hate seeing my baby this way." Tears start rolling down her cheeks, and she covers her face with her hands as she sits down on the bed. "And there's nothing I can do to help you."

I sit down next to her and put my arms around her. I know what she's really crying about.

After a minute Mom blurts out, "I just miss her so much, Dommie."

"I know, Mom. I miss Grandma too."

"And I miss knowing you. I used to know everything you were going through back in high school. Or I thought I did. And now—"

I hug her tighter. "Mom, you still know me. You didn't lose both of us." I hand her a tissue. "You know what Grandma would say to us if she were here, right?"

She blows her nose and shakes her head. "What?"

"Sit up straight."

We both laugh, and we do.

40

New Orleans is its prettiest in April. It's sunny but not too hot, breezy but not windy, and everywhere you go on Tulane's campus, century-old oak trees shade the lush lawns. At any one time, dozens of students are amassed on the quads to socialize, study, or sunbathe. I'm walking across a quad myself when I hear a familiar voice behind me.

"Hey, Cruella. I'm baa-ack."

"Calvin?" I swing around. He looks the same, though a new short haircut plays up his dimpled cheeks, which I never noticed before today. "Hey! Your semester's over already?" I gesture to my armload of books. "We still have finals."

"Yep. Just flew in a couple days ago. I'm working for Res-Life this summer, so they're already putting us up to get things ready." He smiles. "I see you managed to survive without me."

"Yes, but the dorm wasn't quite the same without you around terrorizing the female freshman student body," I joke. Truth is, I'd all but forgotten about Calvin, but it's still good to see him after all this time. I tell him I'm on my way to the library to meet with my study group. He offers to walk with me.

"So?" I prod him. "How was Paris?"

"France rocked so much that I won't demean it by trying to summarize the whole experience during one short walk. I'll require an entire evening to regale you with my stories."

"Uh-huh. Didn't you promise to IM me with some of those stories while you were gone?"

"I wanted to, but I felt bad about coming on so strong before, so I thought I'd keep my distance while I was at a distance."

I'm not sure how to respond to that, so we walk in awkward silence for a few seconds.

"Anyway," he goes on, "you still premed?"

"Yep. In fact, over spring break my best friend's mom introduced me to a surgeon friend of hers, who let me shadow him in the hospital. It got me really psyched for it, so I'll be here over the summer too, taking more bio classes."

"Will your guy be coming down?"

"Who? Oh . . ."

The fact that it takes me a whole second to register who he's talking about stops me in my tracks. I glance down at my watch: 10:12 a.m. I woke up at 9:45. I'd absolutely no thoughts of Wes until Calvin mentioned him just now. That's twenty-seven whole minutes! My previous record was eleven.

"Uh-oh," Calvin says hesitantly. "I said something I shouldn't have."

"Huh? Oh, no. Not at all." We resume walking. "He and I are kaput, just as you predicted, Oh Wise One." I smirk at him, knowing this is probably music to his ears. Weird how the cause of my misery could be good news for someone else.

"I'm really sorry to hear that." He looks at me seriously.

"Yeah, it sucks. . . . In all fairness he's not a bad person, and we had some good times. He wanted to stay friends, but it'll be a while before I'm ready for that, if ever."

"Hmm." He nods his head sympathetically. "So, sorry if I'm insensitive for asking, but have you dated anyone since?"

"Well, I sort of swore off guys. Not for forever or anything. I just wanted to get used to being by myself again."

When we arrive at the library, Calvin asks, "So . . . when do you think you'll be ready to break your man fast? Tonight too soon?"

I laugh at how he hasn't changed at all. "Well, the thing is I'm sort of having a girls' night out. One of my friends from chemistry just broke up with her high school boyfriend, coincidentally enough, so a bunch of us are taking her to the Quarter."

"How about tomorrow, then? Remember I mentioned how some friends and I meet every week to play team trivia? I can tell you about France then too."

"Actually, yeah, that sounds really fun. I've been craving Science Quiz lately."

"Wow, that's the nerdiest thing I've heard all year. I love it. So I'll—"

"But Calvin . . ." I redistribute my books so I can lay my hand on his arm. "Just so we have everything out in the open from the very beginning . . . I honestly don't know if I'm ready to go out with you or anyone yet. This isn't a brush-off, I swear to God. I still haven't totally moved on, so I don't know if—"

"Hey, hey, don't get all worked up. We can just be friends. I mean that."

I nod. "Okay. Cool."

"For now." He winks at me.

"Whatever." I smile and roll my eyes at him. "Just make sure to be in touch about when and where to meet up with you tomorrow."

"You can count on it." He turns around, but then he looks at me over his shoulder. "By the way, that's a nice ring, Cruella," he says before taking off. "Matches your eyes."

"Thanks!" I yell out after him. "It's an heirloom."

As soon as he walks away, I take out my phone to text Amy:

27 min! GO ME!

When I press SEND I well up with pride. After a torturous winter break and a lonely semester, I still managed to achieve twenty-seven whole minutes of Wes-free tranquility. That's one thousand six hundred and twenty seconds! I might even have gone longer if Calvin hadn't brought him up. It's miraculous I was able to check e-mail this morning without hoping for the "come back to me" message I'll never get.

And who knows? If Wes had never stopped loving me, maybe, just maybe, I would have eventually stopped loving him. Then the burden would have been on me to end the relationship. I would hate to have to hurt someone I once loved. This couldn't have been easy for Wes either.

After ascending the steps to the library, I look behind me and gaze at the verdant campus, brimming with friends, potential friends, and potential loves. I close my eyes and raise my face to the sky, letting the sun's silken rays bathe my cheeks and eyelids. I breathe deeply, savoring the aroma of freshly cut grass and newly bloomed magnolias. A cool breeze sweeps by, sending my hair into wild cascades behind me. Suddenly it's as if my heart is fluttering about my chest. I really am starting to get over him! I can feel it!

Caitlin's fast asleep by the time I get home that night. I change into my pajamas and set my hair in curlers by the light of our computers' screen savers. Before going to bed, I tiptoe to my desk chair and log on to the Internet. I'm about to check e-mail when Instant Messenger's "invitation to chat" window suddenly appears.

I don't recognize the screen name, but I have a pretty good hunch. I'm grinning as I accept the hail.

DARIA SNADOWSKY was raised in Greenwich Village and Las Vegas, and has written for various publications, including *Creative Loafing, Las Vegas Weekly,* and *Nevada Law Journal. Anatomy of a Boyfriend* is her first novel.